"Literary sitcoms from hell. Mazza is a subversive, anarchist writer...hardly forgettable."
—*Wall Street Journal*

"Absurdist sitcoms alternating with off beat psycho-dramas and tales of trauma."
—*New York Times Book Review*

"A fresh break away from feminist scenarios of the early 70s and 80s...Mazza's stories zero in with wonderful and frightening accuracy on the scary landscape in which many women now live."
—*American Book Review*

"Cris Mazza's second collection lures the reader with a utilitarian prose into a maze of surprises. Not for the faint hearted, but her energy, humor and respect for her material deliver."
—*The Columbus Dispatch*

# Is It Sexual Harassment Yet?

*short fiction by Cris Mazza*

FICTION COLLECTIVE TWO

• NORMAL •

Published by FC2 with support given by the English Depart-
ment Unit for Contemporary Literature of Illinois State
University and the Illinois Arts Council.

Address all inquiries to: FC2, Unit for Contemporary Literature, Campus Box 4241, Illinois State University, Normal, IL
61790-4241.

*Is It Sexual Harassment Yet?*
Cris Mazza

ISBN: 1-57366-041-8 (paperback)

Pamela Caughie's critical introduction printed with permission
granted from University of Illinois Press.


Cover Design: Todd Michael Bushman

*Produced and printed in the United States of America*

*To H, J, L, and all the rest*

*Thanks Mike, Ted, and Betsy*

# Is It Sexual Harassment Yet?

## CONTENTS

# Preface

## Is It Sexual Harassment Yet? An Introduction

*"Don't you think those soldiers crossed a line?" asked the interviewer, after another recent military sex scandal.*

*"The trouble with that line," responded the officer, "is they keep moving that sucker."*

As we approach the end of the twentieth century, pundits are producing an endless barrage of think pieces about the many changes technology has wrought. But at the turn of the last century many of those changes were anticipated. The light bulb, telephone, and automobile had already been invented, and the Wright brothers' first flight was only a year away. As 1900 dawned, the world couldn't wait for the next gadget, or the latest improvement on current gadgets. What no one expected were the enormous changes in the way men and women think about who they are and how they should relate to each other. When the pundits proclaim that this century has seen more changes than the world had seen in the previous thousand years, they're talking about cars, airplanes, computers, ,space flight, pocket-pagers, the internet...but the revolution we have experienced in personal identity dwarfs all the alterations technology has brought to our day-to-day lives.

We all know the story. Throughout the history of Western Civilization, up until this century, men dominated women at

i

home, in public, and in the workplace. This domination was rationalized as the natural order of things, as God's will, as the way it's always been. At times, such domination seemed benign, even taking on the appearance of a semi-equal partnership. Men ruled the workplace, women ruled the home—at least in theory. Men were virtually unaware of the condescension implied in the relationship. And when that power over women turned ugly, when men beat their wives, tongues clicked, but no man thought anything amiss in the underlying assumptions upon which society was based.

After several generations of courageous struggle, women have forced that society to rethink those relationships and to come up with a new model. It sounds simple enough: men and women should be regarded as equals at home, school, and work, and that public policy should in all ways reflect that equality. But as we begin to figure out how to implement this change, we have discovered that the implications are often far reaching, occasionally far fetched, and almost always a little confusing. If the National Institute of Health gives a grant to study prostate cancer, should they immediately give another researcher the same amount of money to study breast cancer? Should we strive to have an equal number of men and women filling every job? Can someone be sued for talking about an episode of "Seinfeld" over the water cooler? *Is* it sexual harassment yet?

Sex itself should be simple enough. We all know about the body parts men and women have, and within each sex, those parts are virtually identical, with minor variations. We all know how those body parts fit together, giving pleasure to both parties under ideal circumstances, and in some instances, perpetuating our species. The problem does not originate in the penis or the vagina, but rather in the ultimate erogenous zone—the mind.

And that is the zone Cris Mazza's work explores, the real source of all our sexual confusions. And as she makes clear, men and women are confused. What does he want? What is appropriate behavior? What is that line?

The human mind occupies a very small place, enclosed within the skull. At its most expansive moments, it can help explore the cosmos. In moments of panic, that skull becomes a tiny place indeed. Cris Mazza captures that claustrophobia with a dazzling display of technique, but more importantly, with incisive insight. Scientists and theologians may argue about the existence of the soul, but only art can truly reveal its secrets. And as we know, some secrets make us uncomfortable, make us squirm in our chairs, make our skin crawl.

This book was first published in 1991, long before human resource people began to take on the role and title of The Sex Police. Cris Mazza had her finger on the racing pulse of our hyperventilating nation. This new edition is an occasion to celebrate a talented writer, and to cerebrate on the little progress we have made in recent years. As you read these stories, you may discover a friend, a neighbor, a co-worker, a brother, or a sister. And then again, you may discover that you are looking into a mirror. Is sexual harassment yet? Read these stories, and decide for yourself.

*Allan Kornblum*

Allan Kornblum is publisher of Coffee House Press.

# Introduction _____

I was first introduced to Cris Mazza's writing in 1991 through this collection of stories, first published that year. Now, seven years later, scanning my bookshelves, I see that I have eight works by Mazza—four novels, two story collections, and two edited collections—published between 1991 and 1997. And my collection is not complete. In productivity alone she is fast becoming the Joyce Carol Oates of the 90s.[1] Cris Mazza's importance for me, as a teacher and critic of postmodernist and feminist writing, is that she is one of the foremost proponents and representatives of an emerging genre of women's writing that she has termed "postfeminist fiction." The increasing visibility and popularity of this fiction makes the republication of *Is It Sexual Harassment Yet?* an important event.

What is "postfeminist fiction"? Wisely, Cris Mazza does not seek to define the term by prescribing a set of features. In the first of her two *Chick-Lit* anthologies, subtitled "Postfeminist Fiction" (1995), Mazza writes that in her call for stories, the term was meant as an "ice-breaker" not an ideology. And that, perhaps, is its most significant feature: postfeminist fiction does not conform to a set of beliefs about the way women are or should be. Indeed, the very writing that goes by this name resists the kind of certainty, conclusiveness, and clear-cut meaning that definition demands. By calling for postfeminist fiction, Mazza says she was seeking to "stretch the boundaries" of women's writing, looking for stories that moved beyond the clichéd notions of feminist fiction as litanies of outrage, confessional soul-searching, or hand-wringing responses to the injustices of a patriarchal world. The fiction she received, she decided, would define the term. What she discovered is that postfeminist fiction is neither anti-feminist nor pro-women; it is not simply about women's victimization or their self-em-powerment. The women in such fiction are "dealing with who they've made themselves into," Mazza writes, and they are "conflicted about what they want." They don't represent any one type of woman, nor are they individuals; they are cultural personae. Whether the female characters in postfeminist fiction, and in the stories collected here, are seen as confident, independent, even outrageous women taking responsibility for who they are, or as women who have unconsciously internalized and are acting out the encoded gender norms of our society, they are at once recognizable and non-realistic. Readers are less likely to identify with the experiences of individual characters in stories such as "The Old Gopher Returns," "The Family Bed," or "Happy Story," to see themselves mirrored in the fiction, than they are to recognize the conflicting desires and demands that the characters, men as well as women, must negotiate in their day-to-day lives.

As a literary critic, I would classify these stories as "postmodern feminist," though that term does not identify a coherent and homogeneous brand of fiction or a prescribed ideology any more than does "postfeminist." It is a term better defined by examples than by shared beliefs or an aesthetic manifesto. For me, "postmodern feminist" describes the writings of the late Kathy Acker and Angela Carter, fiction that disturbs on a profound level in that its narrative form denies the reader the comfort of easy consumption and thereby enhances the effects of its probing of the unconscious illusions, desires, and anxieties that make up our identities as gendered and sexualized beings. Like Angela Carter's revisionary fairy tales, Mazza's first-person narrations offer a kind of empowerment to the women characters, even when these women are not in control of their lives. Because the women narrate their own stories, as readers we no longer focus on what happens *to* the women characters in Mazza's fiction but on their awareness of the nature of their predicament and of their complicity in their own victimization, a change feminist readers of Carter have noted as well. By also putting us in the protagonist's place and having us experience the pleasure and pain of her masochistic desires, postfeminist fiction makes us decidedly uncomfortable as we come to face our own attraction to and implication in cultural representations of femininity and female desire that may betray us. As one of Carter's characters observes, "There is a striking resemblance between the act of love and the ministrations of a torturer" (27). Mazza's fiction dares to confront the truth of this remark.

Mazza's fiction can be called postmodern feminist for many of the same reasons that Sandra Bernhard's film, *Without You, I'm Nothing* (1991) can be read as an example of the genre. In her film, Bernhard impersonates various female singers of the 1960s and 70s, such as Nina Simone, Diana Ross, and Patti Smith, acting out in a kind of drag performance the images of femininity promoted through cultural forms, such as Motown recordings and ads for bath oils. More recently, Susan Streitfeld's *Female Perversions* (1997), a film based on psychoanalyst Louise Kaplan's book by the same title, is another example of what I call postmodern feminism. The protagonist of the film, a lawyer named Eve Stephens (played by Tilda Swinton), acts out the gender role stereotypes—from the ball-busting prosecutor to the homeovestite who dresses to please men—that, Kaplan writes, "are the major hiding places for the perversions" (15). Eve, whose confident and glamorized veneer hides deep anxieties that she is really a fraud, is a composite character, not an individual, and women viewers, unless they are too invested in the female stereotypes, undoubtedly recognize themselves in her without "identifying" with the character. For the perversions Eve embodies, as do many of Mazza's characters, are "as much pathologies of gender role identity as they are pathologies of sexuality" (Kaplan 14).

If feminism is the ugly, angry face that it has been caricatured as, from turn-of-the-century cartoons to Christina Hoff Sommers's nasty exposé, *Who Stole Feminism?* (1994), or if it is academic chic with no social consequences as represented by the media, then Cris Mazza's fiction would be *post*feminist in a different sense, coming *after* feminism; for it fits none of the popular stereotypes of feminism. But if we include postmodern feminism in the public portrait of this much abused term, then Mazza's stories become an important part of the picture. For the truth is, contrary to these clichéd notions, that postmodern feminist writers, both inside and outside the university, have long resisted the belief that women are all alike, that they share a special and superior moral sensibility, that they are passive victims of patriarchy. While acknowledging women's complicity in certain forms of their cultural degradation, postfeminist fiction is still feminist in that it seeks to expose the workings of what Mazza refers to as a "persistent patriarchal world" so that women and men might come to better understand what they have made themselves into and how that self-construction has been fostered by social institutions and cultural myths. If, as Vivian Gornick has recently written, our age marks the end of the novel of love, that narrative, I am tempted to say, is being superseded by the fiction of postfeminism.

There's an interesting story about my connection to Mazza's fiction which will also serve to further clarify what I mean by postmodern feminism.[2] In the summer of 1991, as I prepared to teach an introductory course in fiction, my graduate assistant at the time, Sherry Brennan, suggested that I take a look at a new collection of stories, *Is It Sexual Harassment Yet?*, for possible material to add to the reading list. Having taken my graduate seminar in postmodern and feminist fiction, Sherry knew that I preferred to teach fiction, especially on the core level, through experimental writing as opposed to realistic narratives with linear plots, fully-individualized characters, and coherent themes. I was immediately taken by Mazza's fiction and added several stories, including "Is It Sexual Harassment Yet?", to the syllabus.

"Is It Sexual Harassment Yet?" recounts events that led a waitress, Michelle Rae, to file charges of sexual harassment against her supervisor, Terence Lovell. The story, I felt, would make an excellent study in point of view. Written in two columns, the story presents his side of the story in the lefthand column using the third person point of view, and her version in the righthand column in the first person. The two versions never quite fall into place. The question of just who is sexually harassing whom is never answered. Is Terence Lovell the innocent victim of a woman scorned? Or is Michelle Rae the emotionally-racked survivor of a barroom sexual assault?

In the end, however, the experimental form of Mazza's narrative, combined with the fortuitous timing of the assignment, enabled us to do much more with the story than originally planned. By one of those happy coincidences that come along only once in a teacher's career, my class began our discussion of this story the very week Anita Hill's accusations against Clarence Thomas were leaked to the press. The uncanny parallels between the fictional story and the real-life drama (the parallels became so intoxicating that one student delighted in pointing out that Terence rhymes with Clarence) gave a different thrust to our discussions of Mazza's story during the next few weeks, and in my classes over the next two terms, transforming a lesson in the formal features of narrative fiction (specifically, point of view) into a lesson in the social, political, and legal implications of forms of narrative discourse. When students who came to class prepared to dismiss Michelle Rae as a neurotic woman obsessed with Terence Lovell found themselves inadvertently mimicking press accounts of Anita Hill (the *US News And World Report* story of October 12, 1992, for example, cited "erotomania" as one explanation offered for Hill's charges against Thomas, a term students applied to Rae), when students heard Clarence Thomas during his testimony before the Senate committee repeating almost verbatim statements made by Terence Lovell in his defense,[3] they became aware of the structuring capacity of narrative, that is, the power of narrative representation to structure our understanding of gender relations and social justice. Consequently, the social and political implications of postmodern feminism became clear to the students through the experience of reading—the ideal pedagogical situation. I didn't need to define postmodernism or feminism; I didn't need to lecture to students about how identities are the product of representational technologies and institutionalized discourses, those powerful rhetorics by means of which we represent ourselves to ourselves and to others. That is, I didn't need to use the language of theory some students find so alienating in order to bring home to them the urgent implications of the theoretical inquiries that have produced that language. Mazza's story made the point only too obvious. As in Mazza's edited collections, the meaning of "postfeminist" emerged from the fiction itself.

Mazza's story opens in the lefthand column ("his" side) with the exposition: "Even before the Imperial Penthouse switched from a staff of exclusively male waiters and food handlers to a crew of fifteen waitresses, Terence Lovell was the floor captain" (197). The third-person narrator introduces Terence by means of his successful job and his ideal family life. In contrast, the righthand column ("her" side) begins abruptly two and a half pages later: "I know they're going to ask about my previous sexual experiences" (199). We know Michelle only through her own words.

The first issue my class took up was the one I had intended to teach through this story, point of view, or more precisely, focalization, the relation between narrative agency (who supplies the narration) and point of view (whose vision determines what is narrated). Students and general readers often think of point of view in common-sense terms, as somebody's perspective on something. Thus, like members of the Senate Committee that presided over the Thomas hearings, students had thought, upon first reading this story, that their task was to chose between two points of view, two versions of the "same" story. Their journal entries revealed that students initially saw Mazza's story as *US News And World Report's* cover story of October 12, 1992 presented the Thomas-Hill hearings: "as a fierce and irreconcilable he-said, she-said battle" (33), although most of my students, like the majority of the public, initially found "his" version of what happened the more convincing one.

Reading the story alongside the hearings, however, made clear the point I wanted to make about point of view: namely, that point of view, or more precisely, focalization inscribes a position for the reader in relation to the story that carries implicit value judgments. Significantly, in Terence Lovell's "side" of the story there is distance between the agent of the narration (an anonymous narrator) and the angle of vision (primarily Terence's). The lefthand column uses narrated dialogue, presenting indirectly Terence's comments though retaining some of his language: "Terence said his biggest fear [when purchasing a handgun] was that he might somehow, despite his professional, elegant manners, appear to the rest of the world like a cowboy swaggering his way up to the bar" (199). This focalization implies a sympathy between the narrator and the character, even leading students to conflate the two at times, giving Terence's perspective the authority of a third-person (and thus seemingly objective) account. This focalization requires that the exposition be presented in "his" column, providing the reader with personal information about Terence that serves to establish his credibility as a witness or narrator.

In contrast, for the first two and a half pages of the story, the exposition, Michelle's half of the text is blank. In her column, point of view is unmediated by narrative agency. She speaks directly to an interlocutor, sometimes addressing this person (who is not a character in the story) as "you." She seems at times to be answering questions, beginning a statement with "yes" or "no," so that her account reads like one-half of a conversation or an interrogation. She goes off on tangents, juxtaposes seemingly unrelated comments, and at times responds as if she has been provoked. In comparison with Terence's column, her story sounds incoherent, even irrational, and it is emphatically personal and emotional: "But before all this happened, I wasn't a virgin, and I wasn't a virgin in so many ways. I never had an abortion, I never had VD, never went into a toilet stall with a woman, never castrated a guy at the moment of climax. But I know enough to know. As soon as you feel like *some*one, you're no one. Why am I doing this? *Why?*" (199-200).

Despite the textual clues throughout that suggest Michelle Rae is in conversation with another, most students read the first-person account as confessional. (This isn't too surprising given that most readers in general tend to read women's fiction, especially but not exclusively first-person narrations, as confessional.) They tended to assume Michelle's references to "you" were direct addresses to them, the readers. Thus, many students interpreted the question above, "Why am I doing this?", as the soul-searching confession of a woman who doesn't know her own mind and who isn't in control of her own actions. Michelle was seen to be implicated by her own words, by her own "point of view."

Yet discussing how Mazza's choice of focalization in the two columns positions us differently as readers in relation to the story being narrated made many students aware that they could more easily believe Terence's side of the story because they had transferred the detached, objective, rational attributes of the third-person point of view to the man, Terence Lovell. Because the law itself is characterized as rational, objective, and detached, their reading gave a kind of legal sanction not only to Terence's version of the story *but also to this kind of focalization.* The third-person "objective" point of view, as it is so often called in textbooks on fiction, is characteristic of realism, a particular *type* of narration that students and general readers often take as the defining form of narrative fiction. Such focalization represents the apparent impartiality and impersonality that, for many readers, defines narrative authority, and legal authority. This view is premised upon a concept of the subject as a coherent, rational individual unmarked by attributes of cultural difference, such as gender, a point Homi Bhabha makes in his essay on the Thomas hearings (240). Moreover, because the confessional is characterized as the individual's exposure of the "truth" about him or herself, Michelle Rae was seen to indict herself through her first-person account of her feelings, experiences, desires, and erotic fantasies.

Mazza's story made students aware of point of view as a narrative convention, and as a gendered concept, an insight that had implications for their reading of the hearings. We noted that the exposition in Mazza's story, given in Terence's "side," functions as did Clarence Thomas's story of his family origins and his rise from poverty with which he began his testimony during his confirmation hearings. That narrative gave Thomas credibility. Although Anita Hill also began her testimony before the Senate with her family history—a story similar in many ways to Thomas's—telling of her rural upbringing in poverty, of her strong family and church centered childhood, this narrative (the narrative of upward mobility, of the self-made man) didn't work for her. (Indeed, when I acquired the transcripts of the hearings a few months later, I was surprised to find that Hill had opened her testimony in much the same terms as Thomas had begun his. Her personal history carried so little weight it was as if that testimony, as well as that history, had never happened.) Instead, Hill was cast into the same roles as Michelle Rae—the vengeful woman, the erotomaniac, the tease, the liar, the fantasist, the bitch—however different Hill's poised and reasoned testimony was from Michelle's racy, impassioned account. Asking why two so very different women could be characterized in the same ways, and why two so very similar personal histories (Thomas's and Hill's) did not carry the same weight, students came to see what Kimberlé Crenshaw has since argued in her essay on the Thomas hearings: "That perceptions of the credibility of witnesses [or narrators]...are mediated by dominant narratives about the ways men and women 'are,'" and once those "ideologically informed character assignments are made, 'the story' tells itself" (408-9). Our notions of male and female behavior are the effects of cultural fictions and the power relations implicit in narrative conventions, such as focalization, that structure our self-presentations in various institutional settings, such as hearing rooms and classrooms. That is a postmodern feminist insight.

Such character assignments function to the advantage of the men. Both Terence Lovell and Clarence Thomas can claim the role of victim in these narratives. Lovell loses his family and his prestigious position, and Thomas railed against the loss of his good name and his family's private life, ending his statement by saying, "I am a victim of this process." Initially, for many of my students as for Camilia Paglia in her editorial on the hearings, this narrative of victimization supported the belief, in Paglia's words, that sexual harassment "is not a gender issue" because men can be victims too. And so they can. But this claim of equity fails to consider the extent to which the men, unlike the women, in both narratives are in a position to, and find it desirable to, evoke the narrative of victimization. The plot of the self-made, hard-working, family man brought down by the vengeful, jealous, sex-crazed woman is ready-made; it fits like a glove.

More to the point, if, as Catherine MacKinnon asserts, a woman is essentially a victim, or rather, is made a woman by her victimization in a patriarchal society, then a woman cannot easily move into the role of victim, cannot be the subject of a narrative she is already subjected to. But whether or not we accept MacKinnon's view of women's "essential" victimization (and clearly Mazza does not), we can see in both women's stories what Hill explicitly testified to: the difficulty of going public. Rae and especially Hill appear to be less concerned with proving their personal victimization than with breaking silence. Hill concluded her opening statement with: "I felt I had to tell the truth. I could not keep silent." And Rae is incredulous when her interlocutor apparently asks why she's filing charges: "Why am I doing this? *Why*?", as if to say, how could I not press charges? Telling their stories is more important than proving their victimization insofar as to be a victim has long meant, for a woman, to be defeated, reduced to tears and pleading for help in the conventions of melodrama Roy Lichtenstein so humorously deflates in his paintings, and the conventions of romance Mazza defies in her fiction. The image of the victim has long worked against women.

However, the point is not to respond, against Paglia, that sexual harassment *is* a woman's issue, pure and simple. The stories in this collection belie that assumption. (I'm thinking, for example, of Jackson in "Almost" or Buddy—a.k.a. Darwin—

in "Someone's Getting Mad.") Nor do we need to set up a choice between the essentialism of a radical feminism that would subsume differences between women to a metanarrative of victimization, and the radical heterogeneity of a postmodern feminism, whose emphasis on difference and rejection of such metanarratives would seem to belie efforts to establish women's collective oppression. Instead, we might ask just what kinds of narratives of victimization are given credence in the general public? "Is It Sexual Harassment Yet?" serves to give the narrative of sexual harassment the same truth-value as the narrative of racism that Thomas so successfully evoked when he characterized the hearings as a "high-tech lynching."

This raises the question of the truth-value of narrative, especially but not solely those that are neither realistic nor about real-life events. In Mazza's story, there is no truth to be found because *there was no originary event.* As in any piece of fiction, nothing happened *prior* to this narrative. The characters and events are imaginary. But realism gives us the illusion that something happened and encourages us to judge the characters as if they were real. Postmodern or postfeminist fiction, in contrast, persistently resists this kind of reading and instead reminds us that if there is no truth to be found prior to the narrated events, this is no less true of real-life events, like the Thomas hearings. As Hayden White has written, "stories are not lived; there is no such thing as a 'real' story. . . . And as for the notion of a 'true' story, this is virtually a contradiction in terms. *All* stories are fictions, which means, of course, that they can be 'true' only in a metaphorical sense and in the sense in which a figure of speech is true." The relevant question is: "Is this true enough?" (27).

This is not to say that there is no difference between fictional stories and personal or legal testimonies, no way to determine what happened (a conclusion which would risk doubly victimizing the victim of sexual harassment). Rather, this is to say that what happened, whether in fiction or in reality, will always *mean* only within a system of representations, in terms of "the narrative tropes available for representing our experience" (Crenshaw 403). Put simply, there is no unmediated relation to the truth. The predominance of realism and its version of "truth" is what makes postmodern or postfeminist fiction seem to have no meaning or truth-value. To paraphrase what Kathy Acker once said of her fiction, it doesn't have a mean-

ing but that doesn't mean it's meaningless. We've been looking for meaning, and truth, in all the wrong places.

Such an insight about the truth-value of narrative didn't
relieve my students any more than it would the Senate Committee of responsibility for determining the truth, but it did
change the nature of that task: from determining what *really*
happened to making a certain kind of narrative accessible,
and thus a certain kind of truth desirable. Truth is not to be
determined by abstracting the stories from all vested interests,
but by situating the accounts within a larger cultural problem-
atic and the representations that structure those accounts. To
give up the idea of establishing truth in the realist or objectiv-
ist sense, as postmodernists do, does not mean we have to
acquiesce in the belief that there is no truth. It means instead
that we must consider the narrative and social relations through
which a certain truth is produced, maintained, reiterated, and
lived as one's own. How does a narrative that claims the authority
of being true come to compel belief? When is it "true enough"?

Mazza's story enabled us to see that it is not simply, as
some members of the Senate Committee liberally concluded,
that Hill and Thomas were each remembering events differently, but that, as Crenshaw writes, "the interpretive structures
we use to reconstruct events are thoroughly shaped by gender
power" (410). For example, students wondered why they never
noticed the lack of exposition in Michelle Rae's version of the
story or questioned the omission of her familial history, or
why they never questioned the lack of any references to Terence
Lovell's past sexual experiences, even when they read that his
wife left him on grounds of "cruel and unusual adultery." Likewise, the Senators and the majority of the public never
questioned why inquiry into Clarence Thomas's private life
(testimony dealing with his consumption of pornography or
speculations about his sexual fantasies) was off limits, while
speculations about Anita Hill's sexual fantasies and testimony
by John Doggett about her personal relationships with men
were deemed quite relevant. If in the end, certain members of
the Senate Committee were able to extricate themselves from
an exceedingly uncomfortable situation by mimicking the
parodic version of postmodernism, claiming there was no truth
to be found, only competing interpretations, at least Thomas's
account was "true enough" to earn him a seat on the Supreme
Court.

What are the implications of such postmodern fiction, which deconstructs the boundaries between reality and fiction, for social justice and ethical responsibility—that is, for feminism? If telling women's stories is not about getting at the "truth" of women's sexual and economic oppression instantiated in cases of sexual harassment, then how can women end the injustice of their "doctrinal exclusion" from the law, falling outside "existing legal categories for recognizing injury" (Crenshaw 404)? To solve the problem of women's exclusion from legal discourse, feminists often argue, women must tell "true stories" of their lives so that the law, now premised upon a gender-neutral notion of the individual subject, can come to reflect women's as well as men's experiences. From this normative perspective, breaking silence, as Hill did, means telling the truth about women's experiences.

As Mazza's story and the results of the hearings prove, however, telling the truth is not enough. For what is true is not simply that which corresponds to what "really" happened; rather, what is true is what is accepted as being true within the terms of a given discourse. The law recognizes a certain kind of subject, allows certain kinds of evidence, and sanctions certain kinds of testimonies that establish what will count as the truth within the legal system. What's true and what's real are better thought of as standards of judgment of an individual's testimony. Having faith that she would be heard within the system if she simply told the truth is what got the better of Hill. As bell hooks points out in her commentary on the hearings, the problem with Hill's speaking out was that she had no strategy, no sense of an audience, that is, no understanding of her testimony as a set of conventions. This lack of strategy is precisely the effect created by Michelle Rae's "side" of the story with its rambling, contradictory, incoherent account (which also undercuts its believability since true stories are supposedly coherent and comprehensible). Of course, the absence of a strategy or agenda is, supposedly, what proves one's honesty and gives one credibility or the moral highground. This assumption rests on the belief that individuals exist and are equal *before* the law, the belief that drives our justice system and our common-sense notion of ethics as well. Exposing Thomas, however, required more than exposing his "true character"; it required exposing the mechanisms by which character assignments are made and sanctioned within dominant cultural narratives of gender identity.

This is what Mazza's story does so well. If Hill's truth seems to exist *before* the law, Michelle Rae's story shows the extent to which truth is clearly subject *to* the law. To the extent that Rae takes on the image of women shaped by the legal construction of sexual harassment, telling the truth in Mazza's story takes the form of playing out, and thereby bringing into strong relief, the system of gender representations that shapes our perception of women and our capacity to understand and respond to their suffering, their needs, and their desires. Michelle Rae's character is believable not because she's realistic but because she performs *in drag*, acting out and on various female stereotypes and thereby exposing the mechanisms by which gender is constituted in social and legal discourses. Mazza's choice of narrative for the woman plays out, and plays up, the "truth" of sexual harassment cases: that inquiry focuses on the character and conduct of the victim rather than the defendant, casting her in the role of the mentally or emotionally unstable and drawing a connection—as Kimberlé Crenshaw says our legal system once drew a connection, as a matter of law—between lack of chastity and lack of veracity (412). That Michelle knows this "truth" is revealed by her opening statement: "I know they're going to ask about my previous sexual experiences."

As more of my students became sympathetic to Michelle Rae, as more of the public came to believe Anita Hill, it was not because of any new evidence that convinced them of the truth of these women's actual experiences. Their changing attitudes had more to do with a change in the way they thought about the relation between narrative tropes, legal constructions, and lived experience. Believing Rae and Hill has more to do with affirming women's doctrinal exclusion in legal discourse than with confirming the truth of their victimage. As feminist legal scholar Drucilla Cornell writes, "believing women cannot be reduced, as MacKinnon would do, to believing their accounts of their oppression. Believing involves *believing in.* Believing in, allowing us credibility, includes the recognition of the legitimacy, not just the accuracy of our account" (136). The "I believe Anita Hill" button that I have purchased since the hearings does not mean that I now know that Hill was telling the truth; it means that I have given legitimacy to her narrative of sexual harassment. For what is real is not what is "there" outside of or prior to any story; rather, what determines what's real is the ability of a story to compel belief, a point argued by Judith Butler, a theorist widely identified with postmodern feminism. Mazza's stories do not seem true-to-life but they emphatically compel belief.

This postmodern feminist insight carries moral and pedagogical implications as well as social and legal ones. If we believe that our tasks as readers is to decide what really happened, if we assume that fiction gives us versions of real-life events, then in reading fiction, we can exercise our moral judgment, hone our skills in making just decisions. If fiction is the mirror of life, then we can judge characters the way we judge people, holding them to the same moral standards. We can learn to make ethical judgments by learning to sympathize with others' experiences as these are reflected in literature; we can put ourselves in "their" place and thereby come to expand our notion of what it means to be a human being. Ethics lies in being able to bridge the gap between our position and theirs. This is realism.

If, however, we believe that fiction is representational and conventional, structuring our sense of ourselves and others and our accounts of events, then understanding the effects produced by certain narrative tropes becomes more compelling than determining the truth of what happened. If all stories—even those that are supposedly real or historical, based on actual events—are fictions, that is, are constructed within and according to cultural systems of representations, if there are no true stories, then narratives cannot be assessed as if they were merely relating actual events in their temporal order. To believe that all stories are fictions is to learn to read people and events the way one reads characters and plots, taking into account the discursive structures, narrative conventions, and social contexts within which the stories operate. This view suggests ethics takes place elsewhere, not in sympathetic identification with another, but in the deployment of certain narrative conventions and rhetorical constructions in our efforts to negotiate the dynamics of responsibility in any social situation. It makes questions of narrative conventions central to questions of ethical responsibility. This is postfeminism.

The "postmodern" view of narrative (if we can even talk of such a thing) locates ethics and justice in the very practice of reading and writing fiction. Teaching Mazza's story, for me, brought about this shift from questions of truth to questions of value bound up with our own writing and reading practices. Postfeminist fiction does not mean we must all accept a certain view of women as much as it challenges us to work through what being positioned as a woman means for any one individual by imagining the possible situations in which a certain understanding of "woman" or a certain concept of "truth" will produce desirable effects for certain individuals. Believing Michelle Rae means changing our question from "Is this story true?" or "Did sexual harassment really occur?" to "When will we accept the 'truth' of stories of sexual harassment?" "Is it sexual harassment *yet?*" Is this story "true enough"?

Since that initial teaching experience, I have had great success teaching this story and others from the collection (my favorite being "Animal Acts") in undergraduate and graduate classes. And recently I discussed "Is It Sexual Harassment Yet?" in a feminist jurisprudence class at my university's law school, using Mazza's narrative to provide law students with a different perspective on sexual harassment than the one they get in case studies, and with a gendered perspective on issues of truth and justice. Other stories collected here confront the issue of sexual harassment as well—thematically, as in "His Crazy Former Assistant and His Sweet Old Mother" and "The Statue Maker," which deal with sexually charged if not explicitly sexual power struggles between male employers and their female subordinates, and also structurally in that these stories challenge the narrative conventions and gender stereotypes that shore up popular conceptions of sexual harassment. Mazza's fiction forces us to grapple with the complexities and complicities of sexual relations and sexual violence. Like the other postmodern feminist works I've mentioned here, these stories are wildy subversive, defiantly anti-romantic, non-realistic, and, yes, funny. Mazza makes us laugh and tremble at what we have made of ourselves, and makes us wonder what we might yet be. Her stories are like the process of metaphor, in Homi Bhabha's words, "a transformative act of the political imagination that makes new connections, breaks boundaries of sense, maps rare sources of sensibility, and embodies other, unsettling regimes of truth" (249). They are true in this metaphoric sense, and in that sense, they are surely true enough.

*Pamela L. Caughie*

## NOTES

[1]The comparison goes deeper than their prolific output. The title story of this collection, about which I have much to say below, recalls Oates's story "The Turn of the Screw" (1972), which is also written in columns with the man's version of events in the lefthand column and the woman's on the right. Without arguing influence, I would agree with Robert L. McLaughlin, who points out in his introduction to *Innovations: An Anthology of Modern and Contemporary Fiction* (1998), which includes "Is It Sexual Harassment Yet?", that the best fiction is innovative in a traditional sense in that it experiments with and plays off earlier fiction.

[2]The reading of Mazza's story presented here is adapted from chapter 6 of my forthcoming book, *Passing and Pedagogy: The Dynamics of Responsibility*, where I discuss Mazza's story in the broader context of recent trends in both academic writing and popular culture that have been called "postmodern" or "postfeminist." In the book, I name and conceptualize these trends in terms of the metaphor of "passing," emphasizing the ethical implications of the ways identities are now being deployed, not just in the arts but in lived experience as well.

[3]When Terence Lovell is first told he has been accused of sexual harassment, the narrator reports that "he wasn't aware that anything he said or did could have possibly been so misunderstood"; in Thomas's opening statement to the Senate Committee, he remarked: "I cannot imagine anything that I said or did to Anita Hill that could have been mistaken for sexual harassment." And Thomas's concluding remark, "I want my life and my family's life back," sounds as if he is mimicking Terence's concluding statement, "I just want my life to get back to normal."

## WORKS CITED

Bhabha, Homi. "A Good Judge of Character: Men, Metaphors, and the Common Culture." In Toni Morrison, ed. *Race-ing Justice, Engender-ing Power: Essays on Anita Hill, Clarence Thomas, and the Construction of Social Reality.* (New York: Pantheon, 1992): 232-250.

Butler, Judith. *Bodies That Matter: On the Discursive Limits of 'Sex'.* New York: Routledge, 1993.

Carter, Angela. *The Bloody Chamber and Other Stories.* New York: Penguin, 1979.

Cornell, Drucilla. *Beyond Accommodation: Ethical Feminism, Deconstruction, and the Law.* New York: Routledge, 1991.

Crenshaw, Kimberlé. "Whose Story Is It, Anyway? Feminist and Antiracist Appropriations of Anita Hill." In Morrison, *Race-ing Justice* 402-440.

Gornick, Vivian. *The End of the Novel of Love.* Boston: Beacon Press, 1997.

hooks, bell. "The Feminist Challenge: Must We Call Every Woman Sister?" In *Black Looks; Race and Representation* (Boston: Southend Press, 1992): 79-86.

Kaplan, Louise J. *Female Perversions: The Temptations of Emma Bovary.* New Jersey and London: Jason Aronson, 1991.

Mazza, Cris and Jeffrey DeShell, eds. *Chick-Lit: Postfeminist Fiction.* Normal, IL: Fiction Collective 2, 1995.

McLaughlin, Robert L. Introduction to *Innovations: An Anthology of Modern and Contemporary Fiction.* Normal, IL: Dalkey Archive Press, 1998.

Paglia, Camille. "The Strange Case of Clarence Thomas and Anita Hill." In *Sex, Art, and American Culture* (New York: Vintage 1992): 46-48.

Sommers, Christina Hoff. *Who Stole Feminism? How Women Have Betrayed Women.* New York: Simon & Schuster, 1994.

White, Hayden. "The Value of Narrativity in the Representation of Reality." *Critical Inquiry* 7 (Autumn 1980): 5-27.

Pamela L. Caughie is Associate Professor of English and Director of Women's Studies at Loyola University Chicago. She teaches modern and postmodern literature, feminist theory, and African-American literature and criticism. She is author of *Virginia Woolf and Postmodernism* (1991) and *Passing and Pedagogy* (forthcoming, 1999), both published by University of Illinois Press. She is also editing a collection of essays, *Virginia Woolf in the Age of Mechanical Reproduction*, for Garland Publishing.

**Week #1**
1. *Meet class*
Who says meeting new people is difficult? Plenty of people will always need dog-training classes. Twenty students per class, four classes per week, roughly six sessions a year, that's 480 new people I've met this year. I would tell them about it in divorce therapy group, if I were still going—what a hostile crowd, glad I never opened my mouth.
2. *Introduce the first cardinal rule: Never accept undesirable behavior. Always reward only desirable behavior. Be 100% consistent.*
    I'll have to tell them what happens when undesirable behavior is rewarded even if unintentionally. I have to give an example. The illustration I always use is when you attempt to get a dog to let go of a sock he's been chewing by trying to pull it out of his mouth: Dogs love tug-o-war; you're giving him a great time; his favorite reward is a great time; so you've taught him to never let you have anything he's got because you've been rewarding him for hanging onto it. One time I had enough courage to tell Derek I was going to use him as an example of this. Luckily he decided not to listen so I didn't elaborate. I could imagine it, though, calmly telling them that Derek thoroughly enjoyed each sweaty, aching, sometimes bloody, shattering moment—especially if I was fighting back, he loved it more. Maybe in

a way I was being rewarded too: a dumpy girl like me with a guy like him? It should've been the same as every other time I've walked past a construction site, someone (this time Derek) shouts, "Hey, my friend here says you got nothing to offer!" Except this time I smiled at him. He looked so much like those advertisements where a job in a generic form of manual labor looks like a romantic, patriotic, religious experience: silhouetted guys in slow motion with showers of sparks behind them. He didn't have a pot gut, his hair was clean, his teeth were all there, his jeans fit, it was just around sunset. Halfway on my way to becoming a feminist lawyer and wound up married to an illiterate laborer. As though all the cardinal rules ceased to exist. Quit school when my nose was broken. His forehead in the dark. Didn't he say it was an accident? But he also took the closet door off its hinges, his voice coming from between clenched teeth, "That was the best yet," snarled into my ear, already full of blood running from my broken nose. Behavior rewarded will be behavior repeated. I can't count the number of times, the number of different ways I've said that. But with dogs some things are easier: Take a firm stand, be the alpha, the pack leader; then instead of winding up with a broken nose or a few loose teeth, you'll win his undying respect and loyalty. Maybe if I hadn't left school. Derek celebrated with a six pack the night I quit. I stopped bothering to flinch. Didn't even duck. And look what that got me: Held a bottle of Sominex in one fist for three days after he packed some clothes in a grocery bag, called me a cold fish and moved out.

3. *The second cardinal rule: Expect your dog to behave properly.*

You'll almost always get exactly what you expect of your dog, if you work at it. If you expect it consistently. Ask them: where else in life does that ever work? Don't wait for an answer. The first few weeks are more to retrain the people than their dogs. In six short weeks I try to teach these people how to live with their animals. Actually the animals had also better be learning to live with their people. One or the other will have to be broken.

Or I could say it this way: Expect what you know you'll get, you'll always get what you expect. Is that the same thing?

4. *How Dogs Learn*

Just like people, dogs have enough memory to avoid what is unpleasant and repeat only what is pleasant. Tell them to think of the things they've learned without realizing. I never go to double features anymore because of the headaches I used to get, even my old broken nose throbbed. And I've learned to hate certain foods; if I've ever thrown it up, I hate it. (I also got nauseous once while doing yoga. Maybe it was because Derek had hit me in the solar plexus with a law book. I thought the lotus position would calm me down. I've never done any yoga since.) I love to play board games—complicated ones with lots of rules—but hate 2-person-only games and hate to play with people who get silly and play wrong then say "It's only a game," or "Let's change the rules." Every time Derek missed a question in Trivial Pursuit, he tore the card in half. I never told him, but there were a few other things I didn't care for about him: he was fascinated by the sound of his tires burning rubber; he thought it was funny to make mooing noises at overweight girls; he wouldn't admit to being ticklish; he seemed to live by a rule that fast-n-loud is required in everything from music to cars to TV shows to eating. Aren't I better off? I'm always where I expect to be any time during the day. I always know what I'll be doing next. (I never suddenly find myself shoved face-first against a wall, breaking a tooth, one arm twisted behind my back.) The people I see and talk to are always those I expect to see and talk to. And they say the types of things you expect to hear. (Never "Get your ass back here, we're going to fuck.") I also know what to expect from these classes, so I don't know why I'm bothering to update my lesson plans. There's nothing new to say. I know every class will be the same graceless people tripping over or being dragged around by their wolfish mongrels. Even the application forms are the same; when I ask if the dog is aggressive, I want to know if I'm going to get bitten, but half of them answer as though it's shameful to admit their dog *isn't* aggressive. They'll write, "We're working on it," or "Not enough, that's why I'm taking this class." This one will be no different.

5. *Praise your dog*


**Week #2**

1. *Review praise*

I always have to review this several times. Why am I still thinking about the guy who stayed after class last week to ask how to praise his dog. He has a silky black-and-white mongrel bitch named Tanya. I usually learn the dog names. (But guys like this one seldom have bitches and usually use names like Magnum or Corvet, Dinger, Suds or Max.) He waited patiently while some blowhard told me all the things his hippy-dog (neck kerchief) could do already, like open doors and fill his own water dish. The guy with the bitch was listening and I saw him smile. I'm not sure if he smiled because the blowhard was the kind of guy he'd like to listen to while having a beer in the parking lot at the beach, or if he was laughing because the blowhard was an asshole. I didn't care. I'd seen him smile during class at all my old built-in jokes. One of those flash-of-lightning smiles—electrical current and all—made me almost start to laugh when I looked at him, so I sputtered and choked while explaining leash corrections or how to control barking. Don't even remember what I was talking about, yet I can remember the smile in detail. And his dog sits there looking up at him the whole time—all through class and all the time he waited afterward to talk to me. Finally the blowhard left and the guy, Tanya's guy, said he needed advice about how to talk to his dog. His dog who obviously adores him. He said, "I was a Marine sharp-shooting instructor for ten years and I was trained to speak differently to different types of people. There's one way to talk to recruits, another way to speak to an officer, and, I know you won't like this, a different way to speak to a woman." Was he speaking to me in the way he'd learned to speak to a woman? Little Tanya just sat there gazing up at him, waving her tail slightly every time he glanced down at her. I could picture them together out at the shooting range, him squeezing off shots at a human-shaped cutout, the bitch licking his ear for every fatal hit.

He said, "So I don't really know the best way to talk to my dog. I guess I'm a little inhibited, but I want to make sure I communicate with her the right way. Do I have to talk in a high squealy voice?"

"Talk to her like you would talk to yourself," I said, which is (I didn't say) like thinking outloud—just be careful. A comment made to myself or the wall, but spoken carelessly in plural pronouns, "We should maybe do the laundry more often. It reeks." Later on or the next day—nothing on his face, no hint in his voice—Derek said, "Get outside and do your laundry." All of my dirty underwear scattered on the sidewalk and lawn in front of the apartment—and some were quite old with stains in the crotches—I've done the laundry once a week ever since.

Tanya gently stood and put her front feet on the guy's leg. He held her head for a moment and she shut her eyes. I said, "There's nothing wrong with your relationship with her, so you must be doing something right. She'll know when you're being phony, so don't be. Don't be a Marine when you talk to her."

He laughed, said thanks, and left. Maybe he'll stay after every class to ask something. But then he'll leave for good and never realize I occasionally think about his dusty, sweat-streaked face, nose-to-nose with a fuzzy-headed recruit, screaming "You stupid fucking asshole." And the flip-side, in dress uniform and white gloves, holding a woman and drying her tears, saying something that seems uncharacteristic, like "I'll take care of you." Then the combination: field fatigues, dirt and sweat, oiled rifle; deep, ardent voice—not scream-ing—saying, "Don't worry about these fucking assholes, I won't let them hurt you."

**Week #3**

1. *One more way to say what I've been saying all along: your dog doesn't care if he's the low man on the pecking order. All*

*he wants is to know for sure. Be consistent in your treatment of him.*

They should know this already after last week's demonstration of the alpha roll. Grabbed the biggest, huskiest male mutt, didn't even wait for him to display aggression—had him on his back before he could think, then straddled him, lowered my weight slowly over him, holding the skin on the sides of his face in both fists. We were motionless. Then I looked up. I looked up and our eyes immediately met, Tanya's guy. Maybe it was the position the dog and I were in, I remembered Derek's little motto: you can't fight city hall when you have your legs spread and city hall's on top. Yet even though you know it's wrong, you can't argue because you don't know how it could possibly be wrong. What is that different way Tanya's guy speaks to women? He stroked her back through the whole alpha demonstration. Maybe in ten years of sharpshooting, he never killed anyone, never pointed the gun at anyone—turned it into an artform, lovingly perfected, masculinely precise.

2. *Getting the dog to come when called*

This can be a big help if your dog is on the verge of getting into a fight. Once the fight starts, though, it's too late, no dog is going to turn tail and come back to his hysterical owner. I should know. In the middle of it, the phone rang—how I managed to answer it I'll never know (one arm must have been free somehow); it was Derek's boss. I don't know if his boss heard him say "Go to hell," the phone was already flying across the room, broke a mirror, lay there beeping and whining until it was all over.

Wouldn't this be a better lesson in class with a real illustration. Two dogs could get into it. The real thing, serious dog business, pull the leashes out of their frantic owners' hands. I always picture a dogfight as a twisting, upright tornado of two dogs and a powerful roar in the air. So it could happen in class, before anyone can move there's a cloud of dust and the blood-quickening sounds of a fight-to-the-death. Because of my insurance, I'll have to stop it, so I have to move in and get a hold of one (or both) by the skin on the backs of their necks. This, I know, is an incredibly stupid thing to try to do. But there's only one thing that can save me now: a soldier. Without a gun, he shields me, throws himself over me. But he's smart enough to realize even he can't stop the fight—all he does is get us out of the middle. One of the dogs would eventually have enough and start to run, the other on his heels, the owners all giving chase. The class doesn't end nor is dismissed, it just disintegrates. So only he and I (and Tanya) are left in the dimly lit parking lot. He touches a wound on my arm, but there's nothing to say, so I still don't hear him speak to a woman.

It would seem a contradiction, though, since I saw him leave class last week in a battered yellow Subaru BRAT, stereo blaring, MARINES bumper sticker on the back. Tanya shared the front seat.

**Week #4**

It's more than half over. Still feels like it's waiting to start. He hasn't stayed after class to ask a question since that first time. When I say, "That's all for tonight unless you have questions," I see him head for the Subaru with Tanya just before I'm surrounded by the inevitable half-dozen with problems. During the times when I'm explaining something and the whole class gathers around, he wears glasses—not sunglasses. He takes them off during training activities. A Marine in glasses. It seems like I have to keep watching him so I can figure out what's so fascinating about it. Does he look at me that way because it's the way good Marines listen to instructions, or does he maybe want to talk to me differently than the way a Marine talks to an officer? Differently than the way he talks to just anyone. Except maybe Tanya.

What's on for tonight ....

1. *Rudiments of protection training*

Teach your dog to bark at people outside the house. Have a friend walk around while you stay inside with the dog encouraging him to bark, barking with him, exciting him to bark.

Might be interesting if I hint or insinuate that there have been several burglaries in my neighborhood, or that I hear noises in the bushes at night, or there's a peeping tom. His shadow flickers outside my windows. It couldn't be Derek again; Derek doesn't know where I live anymore; I won't even mention Derek. Then I'll say, "In this instance you'd want a dog who knows what to bark at." I don't want anyone encouraging their dogs to attack. They may be friendly pets now but with the wrong handling could be turned into dangerous weapons. Then maybe after class Tanya's guy will stay with all the question-askers. As soon as one is satisfied and leaves, the others turn questioningly to each other to see who's next. Tanya's guy always indicates "you go next" and he continues to wait. When the last problem-digger, problem-chewer, problem-licker has finished trying to convince me their problem is impossible to solve—they don't want answers, they want me to agree nothing can be done—when they're all gone, Tanya's guy is still there to say, "No dogs to protect you?" Dogs aren't always enough. "Maybe I could stay with you tonight and scare him off," he'll say.

I should bring an airline crate to class tonight. Tanya will have to have one so she can ride in the bed of the Subaru when her guy gives me a ride home after my '64 Rambler finally chokes out a death-rattle. Amazing that it lived this long—Derek got it for a couple hundred, took it apart three times, cursing at me because he said I didn't deserve my brand new Toyota. A great day when he finally got the motorcycle he wanted so badly. I gave him the down payment. I only got one ride before he cracked it up; even helmetless he was unscratched, as though his skin—the same color all over—was protection enough, the beauty completely invulnerable, all that construction work and his hands still lovely. But the ruined motorcycle—I couldn't afford to replace it. My fault, he said, he'd had to buy such a cheap one. And I had only one ride. Maybe I'll remember it forever: Taking a turn without slowing down, leaning into it like one body, twenty miles later your heart's kicking you as though you ran the whole way. A ride in a Subaru can't be anything like that. But I wasn't given a choice. I'll let him kneel by the window all night with a rifle, although he never has to aim it at anything. In the morning we'll have to decide whether he should come to stand guard every night until the prowler returns. But maybe once will be enough.

Luckily I can teach this class by rote, just go on with saying the things I've said a thousand times before, hardly hear myself saying them.

**Week #5**

How far have we come? Looked around the class last week—they are actually improving. Big dogs sitting, waiting for a command; walking relaxed beside their owners on a loose lead; staying when told. But I don't remember teaching any of it—describing technique, giving individual help and advice, explaining canine learning patterns ... when was I doing all that? I stand there talking, watching Tanya's guy fondle the inside of her ear with his thumb which makes her lean against him with her head tilted back, her legs relaxed, her belly showing, and I don't know what I've been talking about. Can't even pay attention to myself, I must not be a very good instructor. Derek used to say only assholes were teachers. I prefer to call myself a *trainer*. He thought I should get a job as a cocktail waitress so he and his friends could go out and not have to waste so much money on tips. Locked me out of the house when I was fired. Screamed out the window, "What kind of worthless bitch can't even serve beer!" Said I was a snot, that I thought I was too good, a spoiled-little-rich-girl. So I gave him my Toyota for his birthday. I was left with the Rambler, but he never *gave* it to me. He said I'd gotten too much for Christmas and my birthday when I was younger, so it was his job to straighten me out by not giving me presents. Also called me a spoiled brat every time I suggested I could quit punching the cash register at K-Mart and go back to school. There's nothing stopping me now from going back. Derek predicted I would. But maybe I'll do something he couldn't predict so easily. Join the Marines. Tanya's guy will talk to me like a recruit, our faces less than an inch apart as he screams about what a stupid-fucking-asshole-with-maggots-for-brains I am. I'll smell his skin—sweat and mud and canvas and gunpowder. My knees may weaken, but I'll stand stiffly at attention, maintaining that half-inch of space between us consistently from head to foot, quivering but not touching anywhere. Then after the formation has gone trotting double-time down the dusty road, after "chow," I'll come back to the range, alone, and he'll be there to lie beside me, show me how to aim the gun, put his cheek beside mine as I glare down the barrel. That's when he'll talk to me as a woman.

## Week #6

1. *Ask Tanya's guy where I could get a gun, could I borrow his?*

     I know how to find Derek. That little bar where I was a waitress for two weeks. Follow him home. He won't recognize the yellow Subaru trailing him. Derek steps out of the Toyota. His hair is a little longer, a little blonder. He hasn't shaved since yesterday morning. Tanya's guy is quiet and still beside me in the Subaru, parked across the street from Derek's apartment. Derek puts his six-pack under one arm and unlocks his mailbox. I'm moving now—I know Derek won't pause to read the return addresses. The Subaru door blows open, I somersault out, like I learned ... somewhere. Crawl on my belly across the asphalt, crouch behind the Toyota, set myself, brace the rifle over the fender. In my sights, his blue eye—but before firing, I shout. I want him to know it's me. I want to see his eyes terrified.

Derek screams like a girl and runs into the bushes, thrashing around, the mail like large white snowflakes on the lawn. I'm still shouting. I don't know what I'm shouting, just my voice, harsh and wild. Mid-word, I'm hit from behind, slamming my gut and chest into the car's fender, the gun flies out of my hand, skids over the car's hood and rattles into the gutter while I am wrestled to the street, Tanya's guy smothering me between himself and the pavement, the force of his body all over me, and the force of his voice, talking to me like he would talk to himself, "No, no, no, no ...." But I'll have to fight him off so I can run to Derek, to hold him until he's no longer trembling, stroke his hair and mumble so low that the only way he can hear me is through his ear pressed against my chest. Tanya's guy is watching, holding the gun, muzzle to the ground, and our eyes meet. Which one should I love, since both are neither real nor imaginary?

## Week #7
### Graduation

After I hand him his little certificate and he smiles without really looking at me, not even wearing his glasses, and he starts to walk away with Tanya swishing her fanny—maybe like an unanticipated gunshot, like sniperfire, I'll call out his name, which I don't even know.

# Almost

The doctor said it must've been a pinched nerve that caused half of Jackson's body—his right arm and right leg—to become weak. Therefore, the weakness would be temporary.

Jackson laughed for the first time in two weeks. "God, what a relief—it felt like my body was betraying me. I got tired waving for a taxi; I tried to do pushups and fell on my face ...." He was sitting upright on the examination table until suddenly he was lying down, his shoulders crinkling the tissue sheet, his head landing on the flat paper pillow. "Jesus, but that huge machine scared me even more than I already was."

"Until I got the results of that CAT scan," the doctor said, "I would've guessed these were symptoms of a brain tumor."

Jackson stopped smiling.

2

He keeps picturing himself doing things: Like driving through his garage door, the splintered wood screeching against the car's metal body. Then when he has to take a hammer inside to tap down a loose carpet tack, he's careful because he can easily imagine himself using the hammer to shatter the TV screen or smash the front of his 100-gallon built-in wall aquarium. Later, carrying a pot of hot soup from the stove to the kitchen table, he sees how his fingers would simply open and he'd have to jump back as the pot dive-bombed and boiling red vegetable soup exploded against the wall.

### 3

Molly has been his best friend for almost thirty years. They're practically cousins—their mothers had been as close as sisters. He calls her then picks her up and drives to a small, dark, quiet park to sit in the car and talk. Since adolescence, Molly has grown into her large, awkward, loose-jointed body only in that she's added flesh—big pillowy breasts and ample thighs. She seems floppy and comfortable wherever she is. She's almost always been like that: Holding snakes and letting spiders or snails walk on her when she was eight; sitting on him and tickling him when they were twelve; giving massages to the wrestling team in high school. She'd never finished her last year of college, but had been studying recreation therapy, which was enough for her to be paid by the county to visit all fifteen public rest homes and convalescent hospitals each week to lead sing-a-longs and bingo. If Jackson had been keeping track, and if he knew how many cigarettes came in a pack, he'd know exactly how many times he's seen Molly since his wife's funeral eight years before, because Molly buys one pack of cigarettes every January second and only smokes when she's with him—just one cigarette. Then for Christmas every year she sends Jackson all the remaining cigarettes from the pack.

### 4

She's wearing baggy-legged Hawaiian print pants and a soft white sweatshirt that smells pungently of cotton—until she lights a cigarette.

"Your turn to start," she says.

"Are you sure? I don't really feel like it."

"In a funk again? Want me to start? No problem." She inhales, smiling on the cigarette. "Everything okay?"

"Yup," he says. "A-okay."

"Okay as a day in May?"

"Okay as a day to shout hooray," he mutters, looking at his hands knotted on his lap.

Molly throws her head back and shoots out a geyser of smoke. "We're getting older, Molly."

"Yup. Isn't it great? All of a sudden *most* men find me irresistible. It's the rest of you I can't understand." She brushes ash from the seat between their knees. "Smoke still bother you?"

"Yeah, but I won't ask you to stop."

"Open your window, I only have one or two puffs left. And," she says, "after all, you're such a bore, *some*thing's got to perk up these little get-togethers."

"You want not boring? Here, feel this!" He is twisted on the seat, his back to the door, his knees drawn up to his chest.

"Jackson!" she laughs. "You've finally flipped! I love it!"

"No, really, hold my feet, take off my shoes if you want."

Molly holds the cigarette in her mouth and pulls Jackson's shoes off. "Whew, thank God for the smoke." She peels his socks off.

"Hold on to my feet," he says. "Brace your arms." One of his hands holds onto the back of the seat, the other grips the steering wheel. "Ready?" When Jackson's legs push to straighten themselves out, Molly's hands at first fly back until she returns the pressure and holds both his legs equally half cocked, her hands holding his feet on either side of her face.

"Nice trick, Jackson."

"No, really, two days ago I wouldn't've been able to move my right leg at all, I mean it, you'd've felt the difference, just two days ago."

"Sorry I missed it." She drops his feet.

"Two days ago it was really bad."

"So what happened, a miracle cure?" She rolls down her window. "You should come give inspirational talks at the old folks homes." She tosses Jackson's shoes onto the hood of the car, then also tosses his socks there. One lands draped across the front of the windshield.

## 5

"I thought of you today out at Gateway Haven," Molly says. "It was probably a premonition that you'd call." She puts her feet on the dashboard. The vinyl seat creaks as she leans back. "Anyway, they have a big fish tank in the lobby and there's this big slimy looking fish with a huge suckermouth hanging from the glass." With one foot she taps the windshield where Jackson's sock is still slung. "That's what this reminds me of, that big ugly fish hanging from the side of the aquarium. But I thought of you and how you could use something like that sucker fish to keep the algae off the sides of your fish tank."

"I almost killed all my fish today."

"What? Your precious babies?" She leans forward and crushes her cigarette in the ashtray. "You mean your life's biggest fear almost happened this time—your hand shook while adding the water-treatment so you used three drops instead of two, or your eyes blurred-up while setting the temperature and you put it half a degree too high?"

"Worse than that—"

"Oh, I get it now—it was somehow connected to this thing with your right leg!" She nestles farther back into her seat, tucking one leg under her. "Poor Jackson—two days ago when you could do your little trick with your right and left leg, there was no one to show it to but your fish." She smiles, one finger across her lips, then she pokes him in the arm. "And if your fish had been more responsive you probably wouldn't've had to call *me*. But, luckily—for me, that is—fish don't emulate human responses, like pity or anguish ... or hilarity ....

I've often wondered about that—when people say their dog or cat or horse is almost human. The old folks say it all the time at the homes when I haul out the puppy posters. But think about it: the pet is almost human, humans *aren't* perfect—right Jackson, you'll back me up on that?—so almost-human is almost not-perfect, but not quite, *or*, in other words, if the puppy is not *not*-perfect, that means it *is* perfect. But wait, that means to be *not* human is to be perfect, yet anything that's not human but *almost* human is also, at the same time, almost *not* perfect. How can anything be perfect—without flaw—and be almost *not* perfect—*close* to having flaws—at the same time? Isn't close to having a flaw *flawed*?"

"Oh God, stop it." Jackson's forehead is down against his arms on the steering wheel. "I don't want a headache."

She puts a hand on his leg. "I can't figure you out, Jackson. Is it that serious—whatever it is? Are you going to cry?"

"No." His breath flutters, his sleeve is damp.

## 6

Molly has her shoes off, stretches one leg across the seat to rest the sole of her foot against Jackson's thigh. "You really make me feel helpless, Jackie."

"Join the club."

She's wiggling her toes against his leg. Then her foot makes a fist, clinging to his pants. "Hey, Jackie ...." Her toes release him, reach higher, grip his pants again, pulling her foot onto his leg. "I have an idea we've never tried ...." Her heel slides down the inside of his leg, nestles into the space where his thighs meet.

"You're not serious."

"When have you ever known me to be serious?" she says. "But—do I have to be serious? Or if you *want* me to be serious, I could be. Maybe I am and just don't know it!" Her toes wave at him.

"How can you be serious and not even know it?"

"Same way you could be turned-on and not know it."

"Believe me, I always know it," he says. "I may not understand it, I may not want to be, but I *know*." Molly's foot has tipped forward, the sole resting on his zipper, her toes clumsily clutching his waistband. "Knock it off, Molly."

"You don't mean that, Jackson."

"Look, Molly, you don't know what it's like!"

"I'm not as innocent as you may think, dear." Her big toe deftly strokes him.

"No, I'm talking about having no control over your own body, you don't know—"

"Bullshit. You think I *purposely* grew this big?"

"I don't mean appearance—I mean what your body *does* to you. You never had to sleep on rubber sheets and wake up in a puddle of cold pee. You never had to stand up and give an oral report and get an erection—"

"Jesus, Jackson, that's when you were a *kid*."

"How does that make it less important?"

"Because ...." Her foot slides up and down on him. "In those days no one could *tell* you had an erection!"

"See what I mean?" he groans. "I didn't ask you to come out here for *this* to happen."

"But isn't it a good idea—a good way to forget your troubles?"

"Not true." His shoulders are slipping down the back of the seat, his butt sliding forward, his head now below the headrest, his eyes are closed. Molly pulls her foot out of his crotch. She's unbuttoning his shirt.

"Sure, Jackson, why not? Talking to you sure seems pointless."

"But it's not fair," he sobs.

"What's not fair, honey?" She unsnaps his pants. The zipper seems to open by itself.

"What if I don't want to?"

"It doesn't *look* like you don't want to."

"That's what I mean."

Her hair tickles his chest as she bends to put her face there. She pokes his navel with her tongue.

"It's just not fair," he gasps, "that a woman can say no any time she wants, but a man—he gets to a certain point ... there's a point of no return ... a point where a man can no longer control himself, even if he really wants to."

"That's bullshit, Jackson." She laughs. "I've heard women complain that they can't come 'cause they can't allow themselves to lose control. Well, if they really *had* that total control, they could come if they damn well wanted to, right? Now, are we gonna make-out or should I have another cigarette?"

"Oh God ...," he moans. "No ... don't have another cigarette. You never have two."

"But this seems to be a special occasion, I'll make an exception."

"No ...." The match strikes, the sulphur stings his nose. "Molly, I don't wanna get a headache."

"You won't, the windows are open."

"But ...." His head lolls from side to side. "My doctor ... you know that thing with my legs ...? It was some nerve thing, but at first my doctor thought it was a brain tumor." His body falls sideways, his face on her lap.

"So, Jackson, you almost had a brain tumor." She rubs his head like a crystal ball.

### 7

In a clumsy embrace, Molly is putting a hickey on his neck, low sounds are coming from his throat, one of his feet braced against the driver's side door, the other leg kneeling on the drive-shaft lump. Molly has one leg wrapped around him, keeping him from falling on the floor. His erection is cushioned in her thigh, his pants unzipped but not pulled down. She is panting and has to break away from a kiss to gulp air. She touches his eyebrows, runs a finger down his nose, slowly traces the outline of his lips, holds his face in both hands. Then their ears press together like two suction-cups, air-tight, and her voice is lower, slower, seeming to move directly from her head to his, "I never thought I'd be able to tell you ... I always wished you could love me ... always hoped, never dared to hope too hard ...." Their bodies seem to lurch at the same time, pushing his erection farther up between her legs. Red and white lights are flashing, spinning around the inside of the car, the same pulsing rhythm. "We've created electricity," Molly gasps, laughing. Gravel crunches, car doors bang open, a loud speaker blasts metallic garbled words. The door falls away under Jackson's foot, hands grabbing his legs, dragging him across the seat, pulling him out, his forehead pushed up against the rear window. Through the grit of several layers of glass, Molly is visible, getting out of the car on her side, standing in the storm of red lights. There's a tangle of cops behind him, holding his legs apart, pinning his arms and head.

"Any weapons?"

"No, but he's got a hard-on like an ax handle."

His cheek and forehead have wiped the grime from the window. In one motion his wrists are cuffed and he is turned away from the car, tipped and laid onto the asphalt. Molly's ankles and feet—all that his eyes can see of her—are still standing on the other side of the car. A cop is saying his name and some numbers into a radio, the crackling voice answers, pauses, answers, pauses. There's a big dog going into his car. Another cop is taking his socks off the hood and windshield, putting them in plastic bags. His cheek and nose are in an oil spot—makes his head dizzy, roils his stomach. One of the three police cars leaves, nearly running over his head, parting his hair with a shot of exhaust. His cheek is ripped away from the oil slick, his body lifted upright, to his knees, then jerked to his feet.

"You're lucky, buddy. There was a rape here last night, a car almost like yours."

"It was grey. Yours looks grey in the dark."

"You should park under a light."

Jackson's wrists are released, his wallet put into one hand, the plastic bags containing his shoes and socks are piled into his arms. The cop says, "Get dressed and go home."

Jackson's head bangs into the roof of the car as he sinks onto the driver's seat. Someone is opening the other door for Molly, saying, "Be more careful, you could've been raped out here. You're lucky this time. This could've been the real thing."

### 8

Molly doesn't speak on the way back to her apartment. She crosses her arms and looks out the side window. Her jaw set, her mouth tiny, lips pressed together, almost white. She has the door open practically before the car stops. The bottom of the door scrapes on the pavement, is stuck for a moment, then screeches and scrapes again as Molly, on the sidewalk, slams it shut with her foot. Jackson's closed eyes are squeezed tight, his fingers in his ears.

Halfway back to his house, one hand is stroking the headache at the back of his head. Beside him, on the seat, is Molly's nearly-full pack of cigarettes. His eyes only glance at it once. Is there anything in the world that'll sooth this headache ... or will his foot jump inexplicably onto the brake so the car lurches into a spin that won't stop, ejecting the driver headfirst through the roof where he'll find himself swimming a breaststroke in liquid air as he peaks then heads back down toward earth ... or will his hands suddenly turn the wheel, making the car jerk itself off the road, plowing through fences, snapping a telephone pole, then bringing the loose chain-link and singing electrical wires along as he goes over a cliff—*is* there a cliff?—car and driver both outlined in neon.... Or what, in other words, will the gnarl that's soon to be growing in his brain make him do *next*?

# His Crazy Former Assistant and His Sweet Old Mother

Until today the person I've replaced here was a mystery. Obviously he didn't want to talk about her. Once he said, "She went bats, skiing down the wrong side of the hill, you know?" Another time he wasn't smiling and said, "She must've had a lot of problems, a very disturbed girl." He did call her a girl that one time. She was probably 24 or 25, same as I am now, but I think I really *am* a girl. But other than that, the only times he referred to her was like, "The woman who was here before did this or that...," which he doesn't say often because I have my own ways of doing things, and he's about as flexible as they come, or so I hear. His listeners never even noticed when he switched researchers. A good, serious title—researcher—for someone who reads newspapers and tabloids and check-out counter magazines for shtick for his talk show. He doesn't have a *writer*, so *researcher* has to be the title for what I do.

I also do know that this previous *woman* stopped coming up with any good material. And it's so *easy* to find material—we can fill a week of shows in one morning. That gives us all the time we need to schedule and plan his talks for college clubs or afternoon ladies' societies. For some reason he wants me to go with him tomorrow, fifty miles out in the desert to a country club that booked him six months ago. I can't figure out why the hell he wants me out there. I've gone with him before, so it's not unusual, but all of a sudden now I'm wondering. What a cruddy attitude.

She *was* fired legitimately. Nothing strange about that. He said she wasn't coming up with *any*thing, but I found what she was working on when she left: jokes about some rapes at the local college. Fraternity gang rapes—they get the girl drunk or doped and ask if she wants to rest a while before going home, or they offer her a ride but end up getting a quickie in the parking garage before their car will start—and the DA decided not to prosecute *any* of them. The same term the school gets put on *Playboy's* List of Party Schools, the fraternity's national headquarters refuses to impose any disciplinary action, all of a sudden there're three or four sexual harassment charges brought against some faculty members. And this *woman* wants him to do a rape bit. Like a phone answering-machine joke: "Sigma Q rape service, you ask for it, you'll get it!"

I showed him her material today during donut-and-coffee hour in the lounge. He took the notebook and said, "I've seen this," but sat there reading it all, very slowly, much slower than he reads my material, and he didn't laugh. Well, of course, it wasn't funny, not the material, but amusing at least to imagine this crazy *woman* coming up with the idea and *thinking* it was funny. Then, without looking up, he said, "It's kind of a long story."

"Something I shouldn't ask about?" I said.

"You can ask." He looked up and finally smiled. "And you'll even get an answer, if you want."

"If I asked, I would want an answer."

"So, *are* you asking?" His eyebrows don't go *up* when he's teasing, they go *down*. It's incredible. And one of the reasons why I'm never there when he actually does the show—I can't stand the way it's his same comfortable voice (except a little more animated, for live radio) but his face is somewhere else, without expression or with the *wrong* expression.

"Tell me," I said. *Some*one has to end the playing around, usually me. All of a sudden that sounds bad.

"It was just one of those screwed-up things," he said. "I don't know what I did—if anything—to get her started. But this's the crap she came up with." He was still staring at the notebook. The edges were curled-up and brown. The concrete evidence of one of those times when one person's runaway imagination can pile a lot of shit onto someone else. "I tried saying stuff like: Get your mind out of the gutter, and, Do you ever think of *any*thing else?, or, A one-track mind is great for your social life but doesn't work on the radio. That's all I said—" It still seemed like he was reading the material. He wasn't looking at me. I know why I was a little on edge—because it wasn't like us, it was like watching him do the show. His voice was talking to me like I was the audience he never has to face. I could've explained that to him, but by the time he started bugging me about being uncomfortable, he wasn't doing it anymore.

"Then I got fed up," he went on. "I wasn't serious, though, just a little tired of it, sort of wanted to jolt her to her senses, you know? So I said, Look, if you want to fuck, come out and say it, don't use this garbage."

Then he looked at me, and finally his face and eyes were part of the conversation again. "There," he said. "That's exactly why I didn't want to tell you. You'll look at me different."

"No I won't."

"Tell that to your eyes."

"Next time I see them I will. Anyway, what happened?"

"Guess," he said, grinning.

I shivered, then told myself, This's the way we *always* talk. "She tattled."

"Yup. To the station manager. He paid her off so she wouldn't file formal charges, then had a 'private talk' with me."

"Meaning no written record."

"Meaning nobody knows nuttin'."

"Except me."

"You don't know anything either, right?" he said.

"It'll be all over the tabloids tomorrow," I answered.

He started ripping the pages out of the notebook and shredding them. "This isn't going to change anything, is it?" he said.

"Why would it?"

"I mean, you'll just forget it and all?"

"Sure," I said.

"So you're still coming with me tomorrow?"

"Sure, but—"

"Ah ha!" He tossed the shredded rape material into the air like confetti and leapt to his feet. "A hesitation, teetering on the brink! Why just yesterday I was slapping you around in here and you were loving it."

What he meant was our brainstorming session.
We always have a good time. I mean, laughing at stupid
ideas—that's how the good ones shine through. He'll
pretend to twist my arm or choke me around the neck for
a dumb idea. Or we'll have a fake argument on some
shtick and we'll arm-wrestle over it. It's his show so it's
up to him who'll win. But that's all he meant.

"I *knew* it!" he was saying. "Open my big mouth
and you're like a naked hermit crab looking for a new
shell to back into." My arm was lying on the table.
Suddenly he slammed his hand down on it, clamping
my wrist down so I couldn't pull away. I hadn't been
*planning* to pull away, but I jumped and *did* pull when he
grabbed me. But he was stronger. "But *what*?" he said.

"I was just wondering why you wanted me to
go."

"Oh." He let my arm loose. "I just can't face it
alone."

I guess he meant the retirement village country
club.

\*

Naturally I was a zombie afterwards and remember nothing about his act at the country club. I probably
sat backstage, spine erect, knees and ankles tremblingly
pressed together, even though I was wearing slacks.
These horrible chocolate brown pants I always saved for
a special occasion. They're so tight, size 3. I wear a 7 but
they were the only brown ones on the rack, so chocolate
they almost smelled sweet—god, that's sick—size 3, but
they *fit*. A miracle. A mistake. If the sleek brown pants fit,

wear them—but only on special occasions. To dinner, to a party ... to his sweet old mother's mobile home, surrounded by zinnias and petunias and white rocks, second row from the end in the Deer Meadow Rancho Estates in the middle of the California desert. Not the same place as the talk he gave. Twenty miles east of that. An unannounced detour. But she was expecting us. At least she expected *him*.

I kept thinking I wanted to go back and study her first expression when she saw me (in these pants), to freeze time right before the split-second it must've taken her to pretend to recover. But I didn't actually see her face, I was behind him. Was it horror ("What's he done *now*?") or disgust ("*this* again?") or lost innocence ("oh my *god*...!"). She never asked where his wife was. At one point she showed me his baby pictures while he smiled benignly behind her, over her head. She said, "I didn't know you were bringing anyone, but I'm glad I made enough." She'd prepared strawberry shortcake. For his birthday.

"Did you know it was my birthday?" he said.

*How much else do I not know?*

I said, "How old?"

"A milestone. Thirty-five." His mother was rattling something in the tiny kitchen, maybe she was trembling, how thin were the walls between us. He said, "From the look of your expression you'd think I just said *sixty*-five."

"But I'm not surprised that you're 35."

"My mother's not going to bite you."

*You haven't even told her who I really am!* She was coming back with a tray. I should've stood to help her, teacups teetering in a stack, steaming teapot, three plates

of dessert with the top part of the shortcake sliding off
the mounds of strawberries and whipped cream. She
only came up to his chest, his heart, had the whitest
white hair I've ever seen, and her skin didn't seem old—
more like a wrinkled baby just out of a long bath, cleaner
than it'll ever be again. Her eyes, behind glasses, watched
the desserts tipping, sliding, falling over as she lowered
the tray.

"Drat, they didn't stay put."

"But taste just as good," he said, taking one,
motioning me to do likewise. I didn't. I waited to be
served, waited to be *introduced*. Didn't he see what he
was *doing* to her? "Here you are, Jodi," she said, handing me a shortcake that she'd quickly put back together.
She knew my name because he'd told her, as we came in
the door—I'd offered to wait in the car—"This's Jodi,"
that's all, no explanation, no job description, not even a
last name, just some 24-year-old *girl* (in tight pants) he
brings home instead of his wife on his 35th birthday. I
think I was all ready for her to grab his arm and pull him
inside then slam the door in my face, but through the
pre-fab walls I'd be able to hear her scream at him, or
maybe cry, until he came out, red-faced and eyes averted,
to take me home (or to the nearest bus station) before he
could come back and have his birthday shortcake. When
I did see her, he'd already gone inside and she was
smiling, holding the door, so I went inside too, into a
small room that looked even smaller because of the fake
wood paneling on the walls, and she'd hung dozens of
pictures and diplomas. That's what I did, I studied the
walls while they exchanged greetings, but she never
asked about his wife nor who the hell I was, and he never

volunteered any information. He's supposed to be *good* at ad-libbing, he never needs a script, we never write his material down word-for-word. I stared at the glare on the glass in the picture frames. She said, "I have lots more too," and opened a drawer where she kept the baby pictures.

There were only two pieces of furniture for sitting—a soft chair and small sofa. We ended up with me smack in the middle of the sofa, him in the chair, so she brought a straight-backed chair from the kitchen and sat down opposite him, the three of us clustered around the coffeetable where she'd put the dessert tray. I imagined trying to take a careful bite of shortcake, tipping it over, flipping the cake cream-side-down onto the floor, and she jumps up screaming "Whore, whore!"

He crammed another forkfull flawlessly into his mouth. "Good thing you bought into this resort, Mom we needed a vacation, didn't we, Jodi?"

"What!" I guess I practically shouted. He looked at me, then smiled, kept smiling at me. I hadn't even taken a bite yet. Why was he treating me that way? His mother said, "I'm so glad you could arrange it. Are the strawberries sweet enough?"

"They're fine."

"I've made strawberry shortcake for his birthday for 30 years now," she said. She was looking at my whole shortcake, my clean spoon, my cooling tea. A new crease on her forehead? "We used to just go out the back door and pick the berries, but now I have to buy them."

"You had a farm?" The first whole sentence I'd said, I think.

"No, no, just a small garden, and a berry patch."

He started humming, like background music
while she explained how they used to live in Riverside
before it was a city. I faced her and nodded occasionally,
but I was listening to him—I recognized the tune, "A
Lonely Little Petunia in an Onion Patch." We'd done a
bit once on the show using that as background. Something about supposing flowers had wars, would the
young radical liberals (the buds, I guess) be called
"people-children"? It was dumb, so *dumb*. Rose-hippies.
During our 60's nostalgia week. Planning it, I laughed so
hard I had to lie on the floor. I almost wet my pants (not
*these* pants). Afterwards he helped me get up. The ideas
were like popcorn that day. Why was he humming it?
Looking at me again, his mother telling a story about
how he tried to get out of weeding the garden, then he
interrupted her, right in the middle, busted right into a
sentence. "That was a good show, wasn't it? Mom can't
get my show way out here."

"That's too bad," I said.

"I'd tell you about it, Mom, but poor old Jodi
might not survive it again. She might just lie down
laughing till she died."

My breath was stuck, I couldn't breathe *out*.
Hadn't she gasped? She was chewing a mouthful, touching her lips with a napkin.

"I'm his assistant," I said softly. Someone had to
say it.

"No, she's my taster," he said. My mouth dropped
open, but I shut it again quickly (jarring my whole head
when my teeth snapped together), as he was saying,
"You know, like old kings had, to prevent anyone from
poisoning them." Didn't *every* one look at my untouched

dessert then? "But in our case," he said, "if she doesn't die laughing, I know I'm not good enough."

Wasn't she believing the worst *yet*? Obviously if she hadn't so far, she wasn't going to burn holes through me with her eyes and ask if I'd taken a bath in brown paint (or melted chocolate). But, nearing 70, was she old enough to still believe in the purity of her baby boy?

She said, "Good enough at what?"

A simple answer could've cleared everything up—put her at ease, let her mind rest—but he said, "Oh, anything and everything, right Jodi?"

My head dropped, I almost cried on that beautiful shortcake she'd probably spent all morning making.

"Wouldn't that be a good bit, Jodi? Why couldn't you stick around someday and do the show with me ... yeah—we wouldn't even give you a name, just call you The Taster." He put his plate on the coffee table and stood up, hands in his pockets, sounded like he was rattling quarters and dimes (she might've thought so) but it was the charm bracelet he carries there. Once he used it like handcuffs to lock my hands to the back of a chair. We were probably working on our gay policeman bit, after I'd read about a town in Tennessee whose crime rate doubled when some gossip leaked that one of the cops was homosexual. They didn't know which cop it was. Then the cops were all afraid to go out and arrest people.

"Another piece?" she asked him.

She went to the kitchen with his plate. When I looked at him, he was standing there grinning, pouring the charm bracelet from hand to hand. Had she seen it?

Didn't she have a million questions? Where did he get it?
I'd asked him twice. Once (while I was tied up with it),
he said, "It's *mine*. Shouldn't a charming guy go on
collecting charms?" Another time when we were sliding it back and forth at each other from either end of the
long table, he said his wife gave it to him after he gave
her combat boots for Christmas.

"What about it, Jodi," he said, "The Taster? We'll
have you give the okay before I can listen to any caller's
comments?" His mother was already coming back. I
heard her close the refrigerator and turn the kitchen
light out. Was he going to get rid of the bracelet?

"C'mon," he said, "you've never been too shy to
shoot me down. Go ahead, what's that question all over
your face?"

"Kinda dumb, isn't it?" I said softly, the only
question I could think of, knowing she was back, putting his plate on the coffee table in front of his knees, so
it was too late to ask if she was going to want to know
why I don't wear any underwear with these pants. I
can't! The lines show. But I always wear pantyhose!

"*Dumb*?" He sat down. "C'mon, Jodi, if you really
thought it was dumb you'd put a headlock on me 'till I
gave it up."

I expected it, I was ready for it: *he* would put the
headlock on *me*, pressing my ear to his belt buckle until
I bled all over the front of his pants, until I gave in and
said "okay okay, we'll do it," while his mother tried to
cut her wrists with her teaspoon.

"Change places with me, dear," she said. "I can't
see you well with that bright window behind you." I

heard her move around the coffee table to the chair he'd been in, then the sofa rocked and I almost fell sideways *onto* him when he sat beside me instead of going over to her chair.

"New sofa?" he asked. He stretched his arm across the back.

"The old one wouldn't fit in here," she said.

"How about if we get them to put one of these in the lounge, Jodi, instead of those awful vinyl chairs—you always say your skin sticks to them. A love seat like this, wouldn't that be neat?"

"No." I said it looking at her. "The chairs are fine."

"That's why you spend half the time on the floor, on the table, on the windowsill—" He laughed and she smiled. She probably wanted to cry. After refilling his teacup, she added to mine, making the tea rise to the brim, one more drop would've spilled it. "Oops." She continued smiling and emptied the teapot into her own cup. Then the silence. I felt the sofa shift but I kept my balance, eyes shut, just waiting for him to end the slow torture by casually remarking, through a mouthful of strawberries, "Yes, Mom, Jodi and I have to sleep together, in case one of us has an idea in the middle of the night," while I jump up shouting "Pervert, sleezeball!" And his little old mother falls over in a dead faint across the coffeetable, on top of my untouched strawberry shortcake. We bend over her, look up simultaneously to say in unison, "You killed her," our faces close enough for a quick kiss.

She was telling him something about his sister who lived in Oregon, he was leaning back, behind me,

I couldn't see him, but I waited for him to interrupt
again, to start humming "Love in the Afternoon," or
"Mothers Don't Let Your Babies Grow Up to be Cow-
boys," maybe even put a hand on my back—she wouldn't
be able to see it from where she was. He might slowly
and gently massage each vertebra until I felt loose and
relaxed as a ragdoll, his mother talking about his nieces
and nephews and their school activities (already dating,
is that a school activity, doesn't she wonder where it
might lead?). Maybe I'd be ready to fall asleep, smell the
whipped cream and strawberries as my body bent farther forward, my head sinking to my knees, then he
would push his fingers into my armpits, laughing
"Gotcha!" His mother stone frozen, her last strawberry
and picture-perfect dollop of whipped cream poised on
her spoon halfway to her mouth. The sofa shifted, he
said, "Showtime, Jodi." I screamed, "Don't touch me
again!" But he and his mother sat there eating strawberry shortcake as though no one had screamed anything.

# My Priest Story

Around midnight, when I get home, I tell emergency-room stories to my lover in bed.

"Don't worry," I tell him, "this one won't involve a catheter in any way, shape or form, by any stretch of the imagination."

"Okay, good."

"It was already in when I first saw him."

"Not fair!" He curls around me. I feel him hard against my leg.

"Well, it isn't part of my story, so you won't have to hear about it again. But I'd better start at the beginning: This guy came into the hospital."

"A familiar beginning to your stories."

"They have to come in before there can be a story about them. Anyway, he came in by ambulance. His wife was there. I got the info from her and started his chart."

"A fascinating story." He rubs against me; rubs *hard*.

"No, wait. Wait for this story. His wife was a pest. She kept going into the E.R. and they kept telling her to wait outside and they would let her know how he was doing. He was just another sick guy. They usually diagnose his problem 'difficulty breathing' over the paramedic phone. And he was grey so I couldn't tell how old he was. Anyone between forty and sixty, when they can't catch a decent breath, they just go grey and all look the same age. And his wife was that type of woman, with thin hair of no particular color, who *seems* to be taking good care of her figure because she wears pointy bras and spike heels. She kept sneaking into the E.R. and they would turn around and there she was, peeking around the curtain or coming all the way in, clicking on the floor where everyone else goes soft-soled. Some nurse would have to lead her out again."

"Hmmmm." Wrapped around me, he rolls over, missionary style, slowly presses himself between my legs, chews my ear for a minute, kisses down my neck and shoulders.

"Wait. Finally they got so sick of it—her coming in while they worked—they shut the E.R. doors. That doesn't happen very often. Seldom. *Never*. Since they shut the doors, the wife immediately figured the end was near and called a priest."

He slows, listening with his mouth on my ear. Still breathing, deep and healthy.

"Well, it was strictly a coincidence, but the guy did go into arrest right then, so they called a code. That means he stopped breathing. That means: stop everything!" And everyone in the E.R. goes to work on this one guy, two nurses, paramedic technician, respiratory tech, and me, taking notes you know. I write down all the meds and what time it is when they give something. So I flicked on the code timing clock, so they know how long they've worked on a guy not breathing. I guess to know when to give up. And near the beginning of the code, another clerk came in to tell me a priest was there to see the guy. They don't want nobody in here, I told her. She said she'd tell him to wait. What the nurse was doing all this time was intubating, but the guy had a strong tongue. That means she was trying to get a curved tube down his throat because his own pipes were clogged. As soon as it's in they can suction and get the gunk out so he could breathe again. But the hose wouldn't go down cause the guy was fighting it. The nurse was yelling, C'mon, honey, you gotta take it, don't fight me! And saying over her shoulder, I can't get his fucking tongue outta the way."

My lover moves off me, leaves a leg across my stomach, face to my neck, gentle breathing, warm air, no urgency. I feel his lashes tickle when he blinks.

"So the doctor finally floated over—that's the way he walks, bouncing on the balls of his feet, and he always wears tennis shoes. Always in a scrub suit. Hardly ever seems hurried. What the hell are you trying to do, he asked the nurse. Well, the guy's got a hell of a tongue, she said. Let me, said the doctor, and he took over. I couldn't really see what was going on with the intubation tube because I was near the feet and they were at the head—of course—and the man's stomach bulged in the way. Besides, having to write sodium bicarbonate (1cc) at 10:15 p.m. and pulse 68 at 10:16 p.m., they don't give me time to watch. But suddenly the intubation tube was in. Intubation started 10:20, I wrote, and the nurse said, Jeez, how'd you do that? Easy, he replied, I'm a doctor—can you count how many doctors there are in this room? She looked over the man's chest, grinning, she herself also in a scrub suit instead of having nursey white legs and hat. Oh yes, she said, you're some *kind* of a marvelous guy!"

A vague laugh puffs nearly airless against my neck, and under his leg I squirm sideways to face him, to no longer tell this story to the ceiling.

"So, then the suction started, and a little gunk came up white and pulpy in a tube. They save it in a bag to find out what it is later. He doesn't have much, respiratory says. Keep sucking, the doctor said, until he comes. You had to say it, the nurse laughed, you can't ever resist, can you? He was washing his hands. He's still grey, the nurse said. Going blue, says respiratory. The guy's face was blubbery, but he was still pushing tubes with his tongue, kicking them up, and the nurse kept saying he's got a hell of a tongue. Don't fight me, honey, she said. They kept taking turns poking into his tight belly to see if it would spring back to a peach color, but it stayed white where they pressed their fingers into him."

I touch my lover's own tight skin, brown and close to his muscles, robust and full of energy. Bump my fingers down each rib. Now I want to hurry and finish the story. Shouldn't't've started.

"And ...?" he says.

"Oh. Okay. About that same time, the other clerk came in again to say, Remember about this priest in the hallway—he says he's waiting to see this guy. Yeah, I know, I answered, but they're still keeping the door shut."

At the end of his ribs, I press my whole palm against him and slide my hand back up to his throat. I love his long neck.

"Go on," he says.

"Oh. So the guy kicked a tube out. They weren't giving any more meds and intubation had started, what more could I write? Doctor failing to re-establish breath patterns, or Not enough gunk came up to be the real problem here. I will, someday, and get my ass fired. You'd like that!" I wiggle closer to him.

"You're digressing," he says.

"Am I? Anyway, I was about to leave, but someone said, He's bluer, calm-as-you-please, and the nurse said, Shit, he got that tube. Hold this, she said to me—to me!—meaning the suction pipe and little bag. I put my clipboard on the guy's knees. Here—*here*, she said and pulled me close to press the tube into my hand. Hold it up, she said, keep it up and pointing into him or he'll kick it out! I wanted to leave. I had other things to do." Like this: rub my nose and cheeks on his belly. He smells warm and fleshy. He's saying something into my shoulder, sounds like, "What're'ya doing?"

"Breathing on you ... isn't it like a sauna?"

"No," he said, "the doctors. What were *they* doing?"

"Oh, the doctor. Just one doctor. He was standing there watching. What's wrong, he asked. He meant respiratory. The respiratory tech was holding down the oxygen lever long enough to fill a blimp, but the guy's chest barely moved. It's not all going in, respiratory said. Four years of college for that. Where's the suction, the doctor asked. Just hold your balls, the nurse said. She was threading the other tube back down the guy's nose."

I lick between two ribs all the way from his side to the middle of his chest. "Don't stop," he says.

"Okay." I nip him a little with my teeth.

"No. I mean don't stop telling."

"I forgot where I was ..."

"You were holding a tube."

"Oh. Yeah, slippery. The one I was holding was very slippery. I was afraid the gunk was leaking—but I was probably sweating. Also the tube that'd popped out had sprayed around a little. Another nurse came in and said, There's a priest in the hall, who's he waiting for? She started to clean the man's stomach with a washrag—the mess from the loose tube. Get that suction going, the doctor said. I'm getting this all mixed up, aren't I?"

"Just go on," he says.

"Well, everyone sort of talks at once." I suck against his side, testing it, to see if it springs up red.

"Hey," he says. "Pick up your mouth and tell the story."

"Oh. Really? Well, the doctor said to get the suction going, the new nurse took it from me and the old nurse went to wash her hands. Something was sounding FFFth against the suction tube and the doctor said, *There*. He pulled the tube all the way out, something at the end, caught like a flopping fish. One burst of oxygen from respiratory shot clean into him which nearly blew him apart before they lowered their pressure on the lever. Call the lab to look at this, the doctor said, but the nurse said, Wait, no, look! Everyone's head was in there, even mine, with my hand cupped on my mouth and nose. It stunk, my hand did. A dark, wormy blob was stuck around the intubation tube, slimy and pulpy, but whole-undoubtedly *whole*. Not blood or food. It wasn't even *edible*. No wonder it'd been stuck down there, refused to be sucked out. Someone knocked on the door. Get rid of him, the nurse said to me."

I have been touching a falling-off place at the lowest tip of his sternum where there is no hair. I test its softness with my tongue, maybe I could count his pulse this way.

"Well ...?"

"Ready?" I look up and smack his chin with the top of my head. "Oh, sorry."

"It's okay. Go *on*." Starting to sound desperate.

I suck his fingers one by one. Usually when I do that when we're here—in bed—he smiles and moans. Now he just says, "The *story* ...."

"Okay, okay— I got out into the hall and there was this priest. What was I supposed to do with him?" I touch my lover with a fingertip, trace the smooth, understated welling of his stomach muscles. I know this gives him chills, like he does to me. I only want to be alive and not fight it and not worry about it so much or have any vultures out there worrying. I shouldn't've started the story because now he wants to know why I'm not saying anything.

"How much longer are you going to keep me waiting?"

"Until you finish," he says. "Did the priest say anything?"

"Yes, he *said*: How much longer are you going to keep me waiting out here?"

I'll finish this in one breath, *all* in one breath, then when I'm done I'll finally be able to inhale again, get some new air:

"There was only one intelligent retort: *What*? I mean, he was all dressed in a black suit and turned-around collar, and a white strip of satin around his neck hanging down on both sides like a muffler undone, with loose white fringe and a gold embroidered cross on one end. And he repeated, How much longer are they going to keep me out here? I said, Well, who called you? The wife, he answered, and I'm just not used to being told to stand in the hall when there's someone dying. I said, They just don't think he's dying, I guess. That's the end."

Panting, I reach for him. Have to. *Now.*

"No ya don't." He pushes me back with a knee, rolls me over again and hovers above me, not touching me except a knee on either side of my hips, and my wrists in his hands pinned against the mattress over my head. "What *happened?*"

"Oh god, help ... okay, okay .... The priest said, Well, I wish someone woulda told me instead of having me stand around in the hall. And he zipped the ribbon off his neck and stomped away."

I arch my body toward my lover, but he stays out of reach. "Finish," he demands, but he finishes it for himself: "He didn't even care that the guy wasn't dead yet."

"That wasn't the point. Yeah—it woulda saved time or something if the guy woulda hurried up and started croaking so the priest could get in there, give those last rites, and get out to the golf course. But it was 10:30 at *night.*" I flex my hands above where he's still holding my wrists. "I remember my hands were sticky, especially in between the fingers. I yelled at the priest, *Wait!* When I caught up to him, I wanted first to take his satin muffler and wipe off my fingers." My lover's face is alert, at attention, perked sharp between his eyebrows. I want to kiss the crease away. He doesn't need to worry so much. But I'm probably really pinned here until I finish. "So, the priest said, Well? And I said, Listen! We could still hear sounds from the emergency room: a low gurgle like a huge straw sucking from the bottom of the glass, the whoosh of the respiratory machine, and now also the thud of the paramedic's fist on the guy's chest-if his heart won't beat, they beat it till it will. No, they don't think he's dying, I told the priest.

I can't remember his face above the white collar, but the color of it was like a fish's stomach. You see, I told him, they got it out of his throat. What? he said. He *made* me tell him, same as you almost. What was in his throat? the priest said—he was *begging*. The condom, I said, he had swallowed it."

I said the last of the story right into his heart, where his skin is like silk, like satin. He frees my wrists. I shut my eyes and slip my hands down his cool sides to a secret place, not so cool, a vulnerable soft spot where his legs join his body.

He flops onto his back next to me. We lie separate. For a second. As I turn to him again, he says, "And ...?" Not satisfied yet.

"Well, the only thing left is when he whipped my face with his satin cloth before he left me there again. I didn't laugh. I didn't cry. I just wanted to come home to you. So I did."

Now it's really over. I'd seen it, done it, touched it, told it. No one dies from love. I take his genitals in both hands, wanting him and both of us to be alive, just alive, what more does anyone need, but he says, "No, wait."

He's colorless, sickly, and—with his pale, unblinking eyes staring at the ceiling—lets out a long, last sigh.

## The Old Gopher Returns

This is what happened last week when I went back to see my former boss, and friend, Champ Stillwater. I'm 28 years old, and I'm his old secretary. The new secretary smiles more than the old one ever did. That's the first thing I could tell was different.

She's much taller than me, mostly in the legs. Plus she has straight hair and it's long, and her nailpolish matches her lipstick. I used lipstick a few times, but I wiped it off in an hour or two, and the only reason I ever wore nailpolish was so I could pick off the color instead of peeling my fingernails down until they bled. *I* never thought I was ugly—I *like* my frizzy orange hair and thousands of freckles. So what if my legs are slightly bowed (I said *slightly*), I'm athletic and coordinated, and pretty damn strong for my size. No, I don't have much of a bust, but I've got a hell of a well-developed ribcage with great lung capacity. My body does a good job for me—holds me together in one piece and gets me where I want to go. I know it's too late to defend myself now, but *now's* all I've got, and better than nothing.

Something else was different too—the door was shut between the inner and outer office. Champ and I never kept the door shut because there was no intercom, so we shouted back and forth, or I would use the extra desk he kept in his office. I had a little sign on my desk with my name, Tam McNeil, and I used to take it with me to whatever desk I was using. His real name is Merle, but he didn't want that on his door, so the door was blank, but now it says Mr. Stillwater, and *she* has a desk-sign that says Miss Butternut.

I walked past her and knocked on his door while she said, "May I help you? Do you have an appointment? Mr. Stillwater is on the phone." But I heard him say "come in," so I opened the door and gave the new secretary Miss Butteredbread a smile over my shoulder.

It smelled the same, like stale coffee, and his desk was in the same place—just far enough away from the wall to fit his chair behind it, the plaster full of black marks where his chair hit when he leaned back or stood up suddenly, like when I came in that day: he stood up and his chair banged on the wall.

Then it was time for me to figure out why I was there. As hard as it was to decide to come back, that was easier than telling myself *why*. He was my friend when I worked there and I saw him every day, and it wasn't just *work*. But then I left and for three years I hadn't seen him, not once, nor talked on the phone or written a letter. What kind of friend is that? Before I went back to see him, I sometimes asked my dog, since there was no one else to ask (except myself), was he really a friend or just a friendly boss?

His hair was shorter, light brown, sun-streaked, but there was grey in it that wasn't there three years ago. He wore a tie and a belt, neither of which he'd worn before. And he didn't say anything to me.

"I've been feeling like I had forgotten something," I said. "Is something of mine still here?"

He didn't quite smile, didn't sit, and neither did I. When he started to make more coffee, I said, "Let me do it."

"No." That's the first word he said. Then neither of us said anything for a while. The coffeepot rumbled and began breathing hoarsely. Everything looked the same—the bulletin boards, the long row of file cabinets, the bookcase, the small table for the coffee equipment, even the empty desk was still in the office, but it was pushed into a corner and almost buried beneath boxes of books and papers. There was a photo near the coffeepot of a group of people at Champ's mountain cabin. I'd never been there. I thought I recognized a few people in the picture, maybe even Miss BreadnButter, smiling, with a white fur hat and matching scarf.

The coffeepot let out a nervous sigh and the last drops fell through the filter. Champ sat down heavily, but not behind his desk. He used the empty chair near the coffeepot. He folded his hands between his legs and stared at them, watching one thumb polish the nail of the other thumb.

I hadn't thought it would be like this. I didn't know what to do. I read some appointments written with perfect penmanship (*much* prettier than mine) on his wall calendar and rubbed my toe on a worn place in the rug where the door scraped. A phone rang somewhere, far away. I don't know what I would've done. I might've left, saying *goodbye* this time, but then I saw the box of junk stored under the empty desk.

"Wow!" I pulled a crumpled mustard-colored blazer from the box. "I'd forgotten about *this*. Remember when you got this—on Mr. Widmer's first day? Is he still here?"

"No."

"I always wondered if he would last. I didn't think so. Remember that meeting on his first day?"

Champ finally looked up. "Uh ... no."

"How could you forget!" I put the blazer on and it clashed badly with my light brown pants. "You came back with this thing and said, he wants us to feel like a team so now we have uniforms."

He was staring at me, and then started talking, but it wasn't his voice anymore: "Are you here collecting for charity, how nice, would it be sufficient for me to say I gave at the office?" He started for the door, as though to show me out, but I didn't follow him. My heart was going too fast, and it was in my ears so I couldn't hear very well, or maybe it was Miss Butterbreast's typewriter. Then when he got to the door, he shut it, and the typewriter was muffled, and his voice changed again, a mean voice he'd never used with me before, except teasing, "What do you want from me, a job or something?"

So I tried to joke back: "Very funny." I shivered and talked fast. "Didn't I tell you, I work in a kennel now. It only took me four years working *here* to realize I would rather work with dogs."

I expected him to laugh, or at least smile, but his mouth just opened slightly and he didn't say anything. The blazer was already wet under my arms, so I took it off. Both sleeves were wrinkled and dirty, but I don't think Champ had ever actually worn it. Maybe to a costume party at Halloween. That would've gotten a laugh.

"*I* remember the day you got this."

He had come back from the meeting and showed it to me, holding it up in front of himself, then he told me to do something with it. When I asked what Widmer, the new vice president, was like, he said "A dog trainer." *A dog trainer?* I used to talk about wanting to be an animal trainer, before I actually became one. Instead of answering me straight out, he would only quiz me: *what does a trainer want?* For his dogs to perform properly. *How?* By training them, of course. *But what if he's given some other trainer's dogs to work with?* He won't get the same results. *Why?* Dogs can't change handlers that easily. *Maybe that's what he's afraid of.* But I couldn't see how any of that answered my question. Why was Widmer afraid of dogs, I asked, c'mon, Champ, what's he *really* like. A company man? But Champ had become very serious: Don't put words in my mouth, Tam, I'll tell you what he wants, are you listening? He wants a *team*, and he wants the right kind of teammates ... he wants everyone to be the same. Wow, I'd joked—laughing a little—then you'd better hurry and get some grey hair or go bald and I've got to see a good doctor or we'll both get fired! But Champ hadn't laughed.

I stuffed the blazer back in the box and turned to Champ. "What *really* happened at that meeting, Champ?"

He didn't answer, so I went on, "You know, he couldn't have been  like a dog trainer if he wanted everyone to be the same. Trainers don't expect dogs to all be the same. Each dog is trained differently."

Champ took a deep breath, then at last smiled. "That's for *dogs*, not people."

"Why should people be any different, think about it, Champ, why should dogs get special treatment?" That was the first time since I got there that I felt I was talking to Champ Stillwater again. I stopped sweating for a second. But suddenly he said, "I haven't the slightest idea who you are."

"What!" Then the silence was awful—air-tight and muffled and hot—I could hardly breathe. All I could hear was the thin buzz of the hot plate, the hum of a fan somewhere, the faint popping of a typewriter. And my heartbeat came back, in my stomach, in my fingertips and lips. Champ poured himself a cup of coffee, carefully, then drank slowly, and finally looked over the rim of the cup at me.

"You're actually saying you don't know who I am?" I was already spinning in place, looking all around the room, trying to find something to remind him, but I got dizzy and fell—I had to hold my spinning head. I almost cried and I almost threw up, both things I'd done in front of him before, but not this time, because he said, "You'd better go home—where'd you say you live? The dog pound?"

"No!" I stood up. "Not until you remember—not until I *make* you remember!"

Suddenly *I* remembered things I hadn't thought about in years. I went straight to a crevice between the last file cabinet and the wall and pulled out two old baseball mitts. "This'll prove it!" We used to play catch right there in the office. "And look— oh ... they've painted the wall, otherwise you could see the marks from the times I missed." People in other offices probably wondered what the hell was going on—sometimes it sounded like he was beating me up. "But *you* missed once too, Champ, and the window broke. You said maybe I'd better quit before I was fired. What a joke, after all the things *you* broke when *I* missed—like the coffeepot, remember?" What an explosion, glass and hot coffee went everywhere, including all over me. I would've cried if I hadn't been laughing. And Champ—

he was on the *floor* he was laughing so hard. I didn't care; it was a relief to hear Champ laugh. He'd been to another meeting with Widmer, and came back and grabbed the mitts without saying anything. Usually he used to tell me what he was throwing—slider, curve, sinker—but that day it was all fastballs, and all right at my head, right between the eyes, then he asked me if I knew what a baseball felt like or if I'd ever felt that way. I was busy trying to keep the ball from breaking the wall down or knocking my head off, but finally it was the coffeepot that got it, and suddenly we were both laughing and he said *good riddance*, as though he'd only been mad at the coffeepot all along.

I put on one of the mitts, smacked the pocket a few times, then held the other out toward him. "You wanna play some?"

"Those aren't mine." He cleared his throat. "What are they, polo equipment? Boxing gloves? Lacross nets?"

"What the hell is the matter with you!" I threw the mitt at his feet. He picked it up but didn't put it on. He held it open like a book and looked into the pocket. "Maybe I'd better call the police," he said softly.

"Wait! I'm not finished." Not thinking: *could* he have me booked and fingerprinted for trying to impersonate an old secretary—but *would* he? I dropped the mitt and picked up the coffeepot. "This'll remind you—this coffeepot, it was *mine*, remember? I gave it to you to replace the one I—*we* broke with the baseball." For a while he had decided to stop drinking coffee, but he was sending me to the machine so often to get tiny paper cups of tepid brown water for fifty cents, I finally brought my own coffee maker for him. "You'll remember," I said, "because this pot was part of the conversation that time Widmer came to our office. Now does it all ring a bell?"

Champ was playing with his phone. He put every line on hold so all the little red lights were blinking, then he turned off the overhead light, leaving the phone blinking like a police car at night. I even thought I heard sirens. Maybe he was humming. "I have to go soon," he said.

"You're not going anywhere until we settle this." I could have tied him to his chair with my socks if necessary. *Then* he could've had me arrested. I held the coffeepot right in front of his face. "*This* very pot was used by me to make Widmer some coffee!" There was no coffee when he'd arrived, just some dregs in the bottom of the pot. Champ didn't notice, but Widmer said, Where's the coffee, girl, when you're expecting someone you should always have the coffee *ready*. That's not in my job description, I'd said, and he turned to *stare* at me, but what was so funny was Champ, behind Widmer, motioning for me to shut up and making faces.

Champ's cup was empty, so I filled it, then put the pot back on the hot plate.

There's a right kind of look for this office, Widmer told me, people should see it as soon as they step in the door, the right kind of person, cheerful and everything that goes along with it—*smile*, girl! By that time I was mad, but Champ was still making those goony faces over Widmer's shoulder, holding the corners of his mouth out with his fingers, I couldn't help starting to laugh, and Widmer said, well, that's a *little* better.

Champ looked down at the coffee I had poured into his cup, and he smiled a little, so I said, "You're remembering now, aren't you?"

He looked away again, picked up a pencil and tapped it against the side of the desk, his face flashing in the red phone buttons. He tossed the pencil onto his desk. "How about if we arm wrestle—if I win two out of three, you'll leave, okay? Maybe some other contest? Name your game."

"Right!" I shouted and went behind him to his desk, pushed his chair aside and opened the middle drawer. They were still there, in back, a very tattered deck of cards. "Here's our contest, Champ, remember? Poker—the loser had to pay for lunch. Deny these!"

He took the deck from me and tapped it against the edge of the desk. "I'm not denying anything."

"You don't think so?" I watched him shuffle the cards. "You know, Champ, I didn't leave here with some dumb going-away present or a bouquet of phony flowers. I thought all I gave up was a *job*." I was suddenly tired and had to lean against the desk. "But I didn't think I'd have to lose everything else I had here too."

"What do you mean?" He turned the overhead lights back on.

When I sat in his chair, the vinyl seat let out a deep sigh. "Of course you wouldn't know ... if you don't even know who I am .... Then what the hell *were* we to each other?"

He looked up from a game of solitaire he'd laid out on the corner of the desk. His eyes weren't blue anymore—they were grey. I took the remaining cards from him and passed them one by one from one hand to the other, face up. "This is typical, Champ. You would never cheat at solitaire, but you used to get me to play poker with a loaded deck—not so I'd lose but so I'd think I won easily. How many times did I fall for that joke." He scraped up the solitaire game and stacked the cards, so I put my half of the deck on top of his. "Anyway, I got some free lunches, if nothing else—of course I earned them with a lot of trips to the bank for the cash you never had to bet with in the first place." I felt so weak, I could hardly think, my head so heavy, it's amazing I even remembered about the check, the one I still had. He would write checks to me when he needed money, and I walked to the bank to cash them, but one of them had bounced once, and I'd kept it, just because I thought it was funny, also because we never did get around to fixing it ... the bank had taken the fifty bucks out of my account. He was going to pay me back.

I grabbed my wallet out of my purse and found the check, folded up behind some pictures, then I came back to his desk and handed it to him. I didn't say anything, I couldn't, I just let him take it. He looked at it, then put it down on the desk.

"Now you'll remember me," I said. "You'll have to, because of this check ...." We were both staring at the check. It was face-up on the desk—pay to the order of Tam McNeil, fifty dollars, insufficient funds—and in that moment I remembered why we'd never taken care of it: He *had* sent me to the bank to find out why it had bounced, but the bank was too crowded so I thought it could wait for another day, and I came right back to the office. But I completely forgot about the check as soon as I walked in. The door was open as usual—I went right in and found Champ interviewing somebody for my job.

While I remembered, I picked up the check again and searched it, but I don't know what I was looking for. I held it in my fist. It was so hot in there. I thought maybe

Miss Butterbreath was turning up the heat from the outside, to flush me out and get me to leave. I hadn't tried that when she was there for her interview. Then again, I don't remember if it was actually Miss ButteredUp or not, just someone similar who could've been anyone.

"Champ, tell me I'm wrong." I could only whisper.

Then he came rushing toward me. "My Leona! You've come back to me!" Before I could dodge him or duck, he had his arms around me, holding my head still, kissing my mouth—which was still open with surprise. He smelled faintly like the office—stale coffee—blended with some cologne that was barely there, and his sweat, and I was dizzy and wouldn't have remained standing except he was holding me. I didn't even wonder who the hell was Leona, and I thought maybe I didn't care. But when he stepped back, still holding my shoulders, looking at me, his eyes clouded, all I could remember was the way he had sat on the edge of his desk as he interviewed her, and looked down at her, and he was tossing a baseball from one hand to the other as he listened to her.

"If you're not Leona," he said slowly, "then who *are* you?"

"Damn you!" I ripped a poster off the wall, leaving a tattered corner still stuck to the plaster. "See this—*I* put this up, I'll bet you never even noticed!" I tossed it to the floor. "And how about this ... I *know* it's here ...." I was looking for a small dog-eared book in the bookcase. "We bought a Hoyle once on our lunch hour because we argued over the rules so often—where is it?" I didn't find it, so I grabbed another book and threw it— when it hit the wall, some of the pages fluttered free. I spun in place, ignoring the dizziness, then once again spotted the box of junk stashed under the extra desk. "Ah ha!" I shouted, and kneeled beside the box. I pulled out a large brown coffee mug with "Champ" printed on it. "You won this in a bet .... I had it made for you. The next day you brought one for me just like it, except with *my* name." I pitched the cup over my shoulder and kept digging through the box, looking for my mug, but instead I found an envelope of snapshots. "Lookit this!" I tossed them like confetti. "The pictures I took at the Christmas party the year *you* had to be Santa." Then I crawled on hands and knees among the photos. "I know it's here ... the blurry one ... where *is* it? I had someone take a picture of *us*. Guess who your elf was—that's right, *me*." I looked at each of the pictures, not able to see well through the tears gathering in my eyes, but well enough to know there wasn't a single shot of me. "Where is it!" I tore them all into small pieces and threw the handful at him. "And this thing!" I pulled a trophy out of the box and held it like a sword, pointing at him. "Dammit, this is the trophy our team won at the company bowling tournament." Then I stared at it. I had to hold it close to be able to see it at all. I couldn't keep it still. "The cheap thing—it's already *bent*!" I threw it, not lightly, and it fell in two pieces after hitting the wall. Next I picked up the whole box and dumped it on the floor. "Look at this junk—I could probably name everything here and where you got it. Just stupid-ass *junk*." I could hardly see anything anymore, so I gathered an armload of objects and tossed them up, then ducked as they fell around me. "Just junk junk junk, half of it isn't even *here* anymore, and all this time I thought it was important ...." I had my back to him, so I lifted my shirt to dry my face and eyes.

Champ was back at his desk, staring at his coffee and swirling it around in the cup, just like he had the day I caught him interviewing for a new secretary. After she left, there he sat, staring at his muddy coffee as he swirled it in the cup, but he wouldn't talk about her or the interview. He had pulled out a piece of paper to draw a baseball diamond. How could I listen to him? But I remember what he had said: When a guy puts down a sacrifice bunt to move the runner into scoring position, it doesn't lower the batter's average and he'll always have lots of other times at bat to hit a home run ... but in the real world, when a guy sacrifices himself, even for a good cause, he's just *out*, period, so it's not a very good strategy. You know that, Tam?

"Champ." I picked up a paper clip from his desk and unbent it until it was straight. "Just admit it, I was a goner, wasn't I? All I want is for you to admit it now."

He didn't answer. I twirled the straight paper clip between my fingers. "Your baseball strategy forgot one thing, Champ: What happens when the guy who's *supposed* to sacrifice ignores the signal—the runner gets picked off at first, and he's *out* too." Then I pushed the straight paper clip into the bulletin board, as far as it would go.

Champ said, without looking up, "But there are other ways to move the runner along."

"That's right, and you did. Would I have thought to resign and start raising dogs if *you* hadn't suggested it? Not that I regret getting my dog. You know, she's already had a litter and I sold them for $400 *each*. But Champ, you know what? All this time—I thought quitting had been *my* idea."

"That's a lot of money for a puppy."

*"Listen to me!"* All that talk about baseball strategy, and then how he regretted not pursuing his athletic
career, and how I shouldn't let anything stand in the way
of *my* career as an animal trainer, and the only worth-
while accomplishment in life was self respect and so few
of us have a real chance to have it—pretty soon I'd
*forgotten* about the interview. There I was typing and
copying my resume while he looked up training kennels
in the yellow pages. There I was writing my letter of
resignation while he told me how happy I was going to
be. Then at lunch he talked me into buying myself a dog
book, and we looked at it together while I thought about
which breed I wanted to start with, and he listened and
let me talk, and— "How *could* you—did you think you
were protecting *me,* or was it just *yourself*—you took
away my only chance to fight back, what kind of friend
is that—?" He came toward me around his desk and
shouted "Shut up!"

"No, I won't, you can't stop me from remember-
ing *this* time, you can't even *kiss* it away this time, I know
what you did, you bastard, you bastard—"

He was holding my shoulders and shaking me,
my teeth snapping together, his fingers digging into me.
"Shut up, I don't even know what you're talking about!"

Then I hit him, as hard as I could, not a slap with
an open palm—I slugged him. He turned around and
stood there, holding his mouth. I couldn't even hear him
breathing. "Okay, you win," I said. "It never happened,
you never knew me." My voice was surprisingly steady.
"Why don't I just get my papers out of the dead files so
you'll never have to accidentally remember I was here,
if you someday came across them." I went to the file
cabinet, but didn't open the drawer. For a moment I

didn't even have enough strength to do that. Then I saw the label on the drawer, in my handwriting: Keep Out—Private—Do Not Disturb. "Champ ...." I saw he was watching me.

"Go ahead," he said.

Instead of the former-employee files, the drawer was full of stuff, *my* stuff: an old sweater, some sneakers I wore to jog during lunch hours, the mug with my name printed on it, the book about dogs and the Hoyle, the blurry photo of me at the Christmas party, my name plate from my desk, and a baseball from the 1965 college world series—signed by Champ Stillwater who warmed up in the 9th inning but never played—which he'd given to me as a paperweight when I complained that the air conditioner blew things off my desk. "Champ ... no one opened this drawer in three years!"

He was back behind his desk, shuffling the cards, but he stopped and looked up. "That's right, Tam." He laughed a little. "I've been *afraid* to open it." He dealt out two poker hands.

I didn't move for a moment, then left everything in the drawer and shut it. I went to pick up my cards and studied them silently—nothing higher than a nine, no two alike. "You used to say guilt is a worthless emotion," I said, "but when you said it the day I left, I thought you were telling me not to feel guilty for quitting so fast." I put my cards down on the desk. "Champ, I actually came here to ask you, would you hire me again now?"

He held his cards under his chin, smiled and shook his head.

"No, not *will* you hire me ... I said *would* you."

This time he neither nodded nor shook his head. He just stared, his elbow on the desk, chin in his hand, silently tapping the desktop with his fingertips, then he laughed. "I bet you wouldn't really want me to."

"Okay ... fifty dollars!" I smiled, got the crumpled check from the floor and tossed it onto the desk.

## Attack At Dawn

*Yes, I'm afraid of him.*

But he grew up in my bedroom, under a lightbulb. On his first night, however, the synthetic, substitute heat wasn't enough for Clarence. He woke me, 2 a.m., calling frantically, his tiny beak thrust toward the ceiling. He was only a black fluffball with white, like spilled powder, on his head. I picked him up and held him against my neck, his shrill beak in my ear.

I took him to bed. Clarence slept on my stomach with the blanket pulled over his head. I woke first.

Always, since then, like today, I've risen before dawn to find him waiting.

He outgrew my bed. Black-and-white tail feathers sprouted. And around his neck, a fringe of thin silky hackles—part of the show. On his body, the edges of his feathers blended with no ridges, making him solid and smooth. He learned to carry and move his head to help display his large vinyl-red wattles and comb. His call no longer frantic, but hearty and demanding.

And his spurs: They emerged, tusk-like, from the backs of his ankles, two inches long, and sharp, curving up and in. Since then, every year in early summer the tips splinter off, honing them from base to tip.

*My leg throbs. He continues to stalk me. I'd thought— when he left my room—I knew him.*

Morning on any ordinary day—his first call is what pulls my body from sleep. Outside, I'll be aware of the watery scent of dew and the smell of wet rotting mulch leaves under the avocado trees, the earthy compost pile, new fertilizer worked into a vegetable garden, a husky odor of ripening tomatoes or the green scent of bell peppers. I'll feel the cool damp air splash on my face and spiderweb lines brushing my arms and legs. I'll hear any mouse who rustles the weeds, a cat stalking, a bird shaking the heavy night air from its feathers. But I'll always have to remind myself to think; sometimes even the reminder is sluggish. At least, usually, by the time I enter the coop, I'll be alert enough.

Clarence and a few of the hens are usually stirring around in pre-sunrise. The three avocado trees on the east side of the coop will keep the dawn murky, and the natural light is soft. A leftover coil of chicken-wire stands on end by the screen door of the coop, and upright in the coil I keep a five-foot wooden dowel. Feed pail in one hand, dowel in the other, I'll enter the henyard. Clarence always raises his hackles and comes toward me, scratching the dirt, arching his neck and turning left, right, left, right, like his mythical serpentine ancestors rising, swaying from a marsh.

"No you don't," I usually say, keeping one blunt end of the dowel against his chest. Any smile I ever felt, I never showed him. We circle, always facing each other, until I reach the feed trough. The mash looks like honey as I pour it from the lip of the pail, and Clarence eats, bending to bolt two or three mouthfuls at a time before standing to glare again. He'll flap his wings, slapping his sides like whips, one orange eye always on me. And frost creeps up my backbone as I watch him.

*Watching him now ... I'm numb. No ... there's the pain in my shin. As though we're enemies. Is it really him?*

Clarence usually stays near the feed trough, head high, posing over the hens there—they look up at him while they eat, as their necks poke in and out. With unexplainable trust, the hens feed with their backs to Clarence, tails up in front of him. And with the same unquestioning acceptance, they are always ready for him. Upon some instinctive signal I've neither observed nor understood, the hen will calmly lower her body and flatten her back, making it possible for Clarence to mount her—pinching the back of her neck in his beak, one huge foot on each of her wings, crushing her chest against the ground as he presses the underside of his tail to the underside of hers. When it's over she'll resume eating, perhaps shaking a little to put her feathers back in order.

But with me, sometimes he jousts—as I back out of the coop, keeping the dowel like a lance in front of me. Always only a single skirmish, and only occasionally will one of us manage to reach past the other's defenses. So if a stout hit from his spurs knocks me to one knee, how can I be angry? I'll limp around on the outside of the wire. And if I meet his charge with a well-timed kick, and he falls back, shoulders against the fence, I'll retreat outside then also.

*Difficult to recall this tenderly now with this throb in my leg and blood on my hand.*

As I banded a hen outside the coop, not long ago, there was a small commotion: long hen-necks stretched and pointed toward a corner of the yard. Still holding the hen under one arm, I went around the outside of the coop to see what it was, stopped and stared, pulse thick in my ears. A king snake was oozing through the wire with his pellet-eyes on a new family of chicks. Clarence moved between the hatchlings and the snake. The hen in my arms became a flurry of hysterical feathers—that was something I understood.

I took the dowel and slipped inside. The chicks scattered from me like leaves blowing over the ground. Taking advantage of the confusion, I pinned the snake by the head and took it outside. Clarence ran across the floor of the coop to the door, wings up and level. Like a hawk diving with talons extended.

"See, Clarence," I said, poking the snake's face at the wire. Clarence returned the snake's round-eyed stare.

I threw the snake far down into the canyon behind the house.

*He's watching me. Clarence, when did your shiny black eyes become staring orange?*


When summer is ripe, the fig tree on the west side of the coop is always heavy. The hens consume gallons of nearly rotten fruit: sticky-sweet pulp hanging in soft black bags. Along with the fruit, the tree is full of large buzzing green beetles, sitting in groups of five or six on a single fig, sucking the insides out of it.

Last night before sunset, I stayed by the tree for several hours picking figs and bugs for the eager chickens who lined the wire. But Clarence couldn't keep a beetle in his possession long enough to swallow it. Instinct compelled him to show off his food and call the hens over when he ate. So they obeyed and snatched the bugs from his beak. I tried holding his beetles up higher than a hen's neck could reach, where he could look up and pluck it from my fingers. They all stood at attention, stretching their necks up, pointing their beaks at the bug. But before Clarence decided to take it, a hen would jump, snap, land and swallow, and Clarence gnashed at the wire near my hands.

The figs were easier for him because I pushed twenty at a time through the wire mesh. Sometimes they were too big to fit through, and the wires split them, leaving fig-sugar there where the hens could've lapped it up, if they had tongues. But Clarence seemed indignant as I piled the squishy fruit on the ground around his feet. The skins broke and the rose-colored seeds glistened in the last rays of the sun. Clarence gave me a look before sucking the figs into his gullet, then looked again.

At seven-thirty it was almost dark, the feast was over and they filed through the small door of their shed to the sheltered perches where they sleep dusk to dawn. I could hear their muffled squawks and restless moving around as the hens jostled for a favored position near Clarence. A last crippled bug lay on its back, waving its five remaining legs. I thought maybe in the morning Clarence would find it first.

*I'm afraid to look. Stand-off? Or am I cornered? It can't be you!*


I was back at the coop this morning before light touched the avocado trees draped over the eastern top wire, but Clarence and a few others were already out. I could see the 'reds moving against the ground, like dark-backed trout at the bottom of a pool. Clarence was a grey rock statue with one clear orange eye looking out of the darkness. An unripe avocado fell off the tree and nestled in the mulch leaves. The fig tree was silent, gathering strength.

I took the dowel and let myself into the coop. The hens milled around my feet, refusing to move for me to walk. I tapped their sides with the dowel and cleared a path to the feed trough. As I bent to spill the grain, I whispered low to Clarence, "There was a bug here this morning, did you find it?"

He muttered in his throat. I kept the dowel gently pressed against his breastbone while I poured the grain. A fine dust rose and settled.

I was drowsy and watched them eating. Squatting, the dowel forgotten, tucked between my knees and chest. A cricket finished his night-song. The sky was light but the earth under the trees still dark. Dawn, as always, unhurried, not even a breeze to rustle the leaves. I don't remember shutting my eyes. Just for a second! *I trusted you—Why? I knew better!*

Spurs up, Clarence slammed into my shins, at the same time snapped his beak over my wrist. I fell on my butt, but I got the dowel in front of me and pushed him backwards, hard. He toppled onto one wing.

Only moments ago.

Now on my feet again, but I haven't retreated.

*This isn't going to happen, Clarence, not with me. You know this isn't the way we do things. Stop it. Please stop.*

Neck stretched, head near the ground, bobbing, jerking up then down. Hackles standing in a pointed circle around his neck, a black-and-white sunflower with an angry face. War feathers. The voice barely audible, a growl, a grim moan. Rocking back and forth, shifting his weight, the spurs freshly honed, long and curved, legs stiff, now side-stepping, circling, glaring, approaching, breath puffing, hissing. *What do you want? What're you doing! Stay away from me.* Get back! Wings held out, feathers separate and spread and rigid like a fringe of spears, tripling his size, getting nearer, coming closer, the violent-red comb the only color ... anywhere.

*You're not even you anymore!*

I swing the dowel like an ax and feel the thud as it meets the side of his head, on his red earlobe.

Clarence's neck jerks sideways, down over his wing as though he's trying to tuck his head under. He falls to one side, one wing flapping, his crooked body thrashing in circles in the henyard dust.

I fall after him, again feeling my bruised legs. He flops, dragging his feet toes-down behind him. The rhythm slows. Slows. He stops beating. I take him and hold him against my neck. *I've killed you. I wish I never saw that snake, wish I waited for you to have a chance at it.*

He does not struggle in my embrace. Against my ear I hear his rough breathing. I rub his comb between my fingers. My blood smeared across one of my wrists, his drips down my other arm. I hold him between my knees, pat him all over and make blood fingerprints on his granite feathers.

Clarence trembles.

Leaning away from him, I stand him up and hold him there. Both eyes open now, he blinks at me. Orange. His tail is up, stiff. He doesn't move.

I reach out a red-spattered hand—a beak-shaped gash on my wrist—touch his neck, his head, his comb and hot wattles, his hard narrow back, his high chest. No resistance. I pull him close to me again, but he moves away with one unsteady step.

His head is up, his tail is up. We stare at each other. My legs ache, I feel my pulse there, but I stand and step backwards. Clarence watches me.

He looks, and I look back.

Again I step backwards, and again. Each step a thousand pounds on my legs. I retrieve the pail and the dowel and retreat, still backwards, out the door.

We look at each other. Through wire.

Clarence remains, as before, a grey statue. The sun still waits behind the eastern hills—they are outlined in flame.

I don't put the dowel into the coil of wire beside the door—it's still in my hand as I leave. No sound from Clarence. Next to the cellar door I place the dowel across two stones and step in the middle. It cracks into a V. The cellar is dry and dark and musty. Dusty bottles of wine on their sides in a crate. Crock jars of olives being processed. A newly painted chair on the workbench. Brushes in turpentine. Rat traps hanging in rows. Rubber aprons and metal tubs, an ax, burlap sacks, a top-loading freezer. I can hear the hens quibble as they eat. Are they looking at him? In the cluster of tools inside the cellar door, I find an old corn broom, worn away on one side, too soft now even for dusting a blanket. Fit only for a scarecrow.

Sparrows are stealing in and out of the large mesh wire. Doves in the avocado trees stir then are silent again, but a mockingbird calls. A hen pauses in front of

Clarence, lowering her head a little, waiting, but he glides past her, head up, like a seahorse. I put the broom into the empty coil of wire, bristles up.

# The Family Bed

Afterwards he left the house and walked down the street. He'd tried explaining to the kid: why continue playing the game when it's a lost cause for your opponent—that's like torture. Finally he'd had to slap the kid and send him to bed.

They hadn't lived here long and so far he'd only walked around the block. This time he turned left then right then left again. The road lost its sidewalk and he was walking through tumbleweeds. It was summer and his legs were bare, so he stepped into the street and walked in the gutter. The road was on the rim of a canyon which was why the only houses were on the other side of the street. The houses were small and the yards weedy. Not that his house was spacious and grand. He'd lost another job and this was all he could do until he could find something better than delivery-boy for a print shop. "Don't worry, Dale," Muriel had said, "Barney's so smart—when he grows up he'll finish high school and go to college and have a lot of money!" Dale scooped up a handful of pebbles and started throwing them one by one into the canyon. "Look at him," Muriel kept saying. "Look at him count the money and make change, he does all the figuring in his head. If he doesn't become a movie star, he'll be a big businessman." Dale had to put his hands over his ears or go deaf. Muriel had found the faded, tattered Monopoly game on a shelf in

one of the closets of their rental house. "Throw it out,"
Dale had said, hardly glancing at it. He was busy putting
the bed frame together. "Barney loves it," she said,
"look, he already has all the squares memorized, he
knows how much rent you owe without having to look
on the card!"

"Okay, okay, Jesus Christ!" Dale shouted.

They'd sold everything before moving here, but
Muriel wouldn't part with her bed—a queen-size with
a sagging mattress and a walnut headboard that needed
refinishing. They'd bought the bed in the first place at
the Salvation Army. He woke up stiff every morning.
The kid slept in the living room on a loveseat they'd
found in the back yard. He kept the Monopoly game
beside him on the floor at night, or sometimes he pushed
the box under the couch if it was one of the days Dale
threatened to get rid of it. Like tonight.

Muriel had sobbed, "You're teaching him to be a
quitter."

"Hey—everyone needs to know when to duck
out." He might've hit her too if she hadn't flung herself
onto the bed, or if he'd ever hit her even once before.

Dale scooped up another bunch of pebbles and
threw the whole handful. The rocks spattered into the
leaves of a pepper tree growing down the side of the
canyon.

"Hey you!" someone called from one of the houses
across the street.

Dale turned. "Can't a man take a walk without
being yelled at," he shouted back.

"Come over here—we're having a party!"

She wasn't exactly pretty. Red hair like her head
was on fire. That's all he could see from across the street.

She was standing on the porch barefooted. When he started crossing the lawn he saw her huge nose and mouth. She laughed. "Come on, come on, the more the merrier!"

"Who is it," said someone inside the house.

"Someone else to help us celebrate."

"What could you possibly have to celebrate," Dale said. He looked past them into the dim living room.

The redheaded woman danced in a circle around him on the porch, then took his arm and led him inside. At first the room appeared to be furnished, but as his eyes adjusted he saw there were only old wooden crates used for tables and shelves, posters taped to the walls, flowers that grew as weeds in the canyon arranged in jars. For a sofa there were two or three large, faded, lumpy pillows propped against a wall, and two or three more pillows on the floor in front.

"I don't have furniture, but at least I don't have junk," Dale said.

"Huh?" said the redhead. "Come on ... come on and meet everyone."

The other two women in the room weren't any better. One had sooty black hair about a half inch long except on her brow where it was slightly longer, greasy, and combed into a point between her eyes. She also had a million freckles which didn't seem to match the color of her hair. The other was very short and very fat, wearing white shorts that cut into her pink thighs, making a bulging V between her legs. She had a husky low voice.

"I'm the talented one in the act," the fatty said. She handed him a drink which tasted like tap water.

"That's what we let her believe," said the red-head, still holding Dale's arm.

"Don't tell me *you're* actors," Dale said.

"Comics," said the freckly one. "We work little nightclubs and vegetarian restaurants."

"Haven't you ever heard of us?" the fatty said. "The Hot Flashes. Gosh, we plaster our posters all over town."

"Thank God I haven't lived here long."

"Huh? Well, come on girls—let's give him a free introductory show!" They lined up, the fat one in the middle, arms across each other's shoulders and began doing a can-can dance while the fat one sang a wild melody and the other two provided percussion sound effects.

"Hi, what's going on out here?" A tall, sweaty young man was coming out of a dark hall. He was gaunt and looked like he hadn't shaved in three or four days, and there were purplish lines beneath his eyes. The sweat circles under his arms extended all the way down both sides, and he had a red rag tied around his head which was also soaked.

"Don't tell me you raise pigs back there in your bedroom," Dale said.

The sweaty man stared. The three girls broke up their act. "He's joining the party," the redhead said, "helping us celebrate— but we haven't told him yet!"

"Oh!" The sweaty man smiled. "Glad to meecha. My name's Danson. Come on back and meet Rhonda."

Dale followed the sweaty man down the dark hall. The three comics fell in behind, single file. "Who's goosin' me," the freckly one said.

"Pass it on."

Someone pinched Dale's behind. "Knock it off!" Dale turned and the fatty smiled at him.

Then they were at the doorway of the bedroom. All the windows were open but it was much hotter than the rest of the house. It smelled of heavy sweat and dirty clothes, and a hugely pregnant girl was on the bed, naked from the waist down, her legs spread. Her pubic hair was soaked, as was the dingy towel she was lying on. There was a plastic bowl with some cloudy water steaming near her feet. "Hi," she gasped, then smiled. She leaned to her side so she could raise one arm and wave. Before anyone could say anything else, the girl's smile rippled and her eyes almost disappeared as she squeezed them shut. Her whole face strained. When her eyes appeared again, she began panting, and she repeated the smile. "Thanks for coming, all of you."

Dale held his nose. "Wouldn't you rather be in a clean hospital?"

"Nope." She continued smiling, then grimaced and shut her eyes. Dale shrugged.

"We've performed at grand openings before," the redhead said, "but this is the best."

"Can you see his head yet," the girl gasped.

"Not quite." The sweaty man poked between her legs with his finger while he bent and squinted.

"Get your glasses, Danny," the girl said. She groaned and smiled.

"You have any air freshener around here?" Dale asked. No one seemed to hear him. "Hey, if this is a party, how about something to eat?"

"Do we have any peanut butter left?" the girl asked, laughing.

"I don't think so." Everyone laughed, except Dale. He turned to go back down the hall and the three

comics also trouped back into the living room, singing a
Scotch army song through their noses. Muriel said the
kid had a singing voice and wanted to buy him lessons—she said she'd get a job to pay for them. "I'm
already going deaf as it is," Dale had to tell her again. He
picked up his drink from one of the tables made of
wooden crates. "Do you have something I could add to
this?" he asked. "It tastes like water."

"It *is* water," the freckly one said, "anything
wrong with *that*?" She was glaring at him so he glared
back.

"Yes—it tastes like shit, just like all the water in
this lousy city."

"You think booze is going to be any gentler on
your guts?"

"Yeah, that's right, immediately assume I'm a
boozer just because I got laid off and— Maybe I wanted
milk, didja ever consider that?"

"Milk is for cows. Maybe I *should've* considered
that!" From the bedroom came a shriek, then laughter.

"Look, weirdo, I didn't invite myself here. I
thought if we were going to be neighbors— but I can see
you don't have a hospitable bone in your body ... or
should I say freckle on your face—"

"Who invitedthis racist sexist bastard in here—"

"Hey," the sweaty man ran halfway down the
hall. "Knock off the shouting, Rhonda can't concentrate." He didn't wait for an answer. The freckly comic
turned her back and began staring at a wall.

"Jeez." Dale shook his head.

"I've just got to go out," the redhead said. "I've
got to keep telling people. If I can't find any people, I'll
tell the canyon, the rocks and trees. Everything has to
know and share what's happening here."

"Why don't you go tell those two what's happening here," Dale said. *"They're* responsible."

The redhead stopped humming and said, "What's that supposed to mean?"

"Look," Dale said, approaching her, "you invited me here—how about taking care of me before you go out looking for someone else already."

"Huh?" She scratched her leg. Her skin was chalky and flaked off. "You're here to share with Rhonda."

"Rhonda has nothing I want."

The redhead slapped his face, then went out, slamming the door. Dale jerked the door open and shouted, "Can't a guy come to a party and at least expect a handful of peanuts for his trouble?" She was singing, and her voice grew louder as she crossed the street and stood on the edge of the canyon. She was singing "Waltzing Matilda."

Dale came back into the room and flopped onto the big pillows. Just once he and Muriel and the kid had started a pillow fight, and he'd knocked the kid clear off his feet, but then Muriel and the kid had ganged up on him from two sides, so he went out and watched T.V. That was when they had a T.V. The fatty sat beside Dale and touched his arm. "You know, this is the best thing that ever happened to Rhonda. She couldn't get a job so she slept around. If she didn't get picked up, she had no where to go, then when she was sixteen she met Danson."

"You mean *he* has a job?"

The freckly girl turned and sat abruptly on the floor in a lotus position with her eyes shut, and she began to hum. The fatty picked up Dale's glass. "I'll go look for a slice of orange for you."

Dale glanced about. There wasn't much light in the room. In fact, the only light came from an aquarium which was bubbling on a rickety table in one corner. The whole table vibrated because of the noisy motor which ran the air pump. Next to the pillows was a bookcase made of bricks and boards. Most of the books were paperbacks which had been opened so many times the titles could no longer be read on the spines. Muriel kept getting books at yard sales for the kid. "He reads like he's in high school and he's only ten! He reads better'n us!" How many times had he told her to stop squealing in his ear before he went deaf. He pulled the books out one by one to see the titles. *Health for the Millions, Diet for a Small Planet, The Making of King Kong, The Family Bed, Fasting Can Save Your Life.* There was one hardback, a coffeetable book with a padded cover, *The History of Southern California.* Someone had penciled 50¢ on the inside cover. Dale leaned back and opened that book on his knees. The fatty came back into the room. "Oh, let me show you something in that book." She handed him the water which now had a slice of lemon attached to the rim. "Look," she started fluttering pages with her thumb. "Here it is, look at this, isn't this incredible ... for entertainment the early settlers used to capture a bear and chain it to a post then make it defend itself against a long-horned bull."

Dale looked into the fatty's eyes for a moment.

"Isn't that terrible?" she said.

"Come on, let's dance."

"What do you think of this idea," the fatty said. "We're going to ask Rhonda to join The Hot Flashes for our next gig."

"You think you can get people to *pay* to see her do this?"

The fatty was sitting crosslegged on the floor near Dale's feet. "I'm going to ignore that," she said. She turned a few more pages of the book. "There used to be herds of deer around here," she said softly. When she closed the book it sounded as though the covers creaked, but it was only another moan from the bedroom.

"Come on," Dale said.

"I heard that sparring deer can get their antlers caught together and then starve," the freckly one said, opening her eyes.

"Ugh." The fatty shivered. "But when you think about it, that's okay because it's natural. The other is ... well, naturally, horrifying."

"It's also natural for a guy to want to have a little fun at a party," Dale said.

"Aren't you having fun?"

The girl in the bedroom screamed, a scream that seemed to go on for hours. Then Dale could hear her panting and she said, "That was a *good* one, Danny."

"Come on, come on!" Dale said. He stood and pulled the fatty to her feet. Her head only came to his chest. Her stomach was touching his groin. "How about putting on some music we can dance to, Janey," Dale said to the freckly one. She shut her eyes again. Dale shrugged. He put both his hands between the fatty's shoulder blades and pulled her as close as possible. The fatty began to hum "The Tennessee Waltz" and Dale swayed with the music, rocking from one foot to the other. "Can't you follow me?" he said.

"You're not with the rhythm."

"Hell with the rhythm." He let his hands move down her back and slip under her T-shirt. He kneaded the rolls of flesh just above her buttock. She didn't yelp even when he pinched her a few times. But the girl in the bedroom began screaming again, and this time didn't stop. Her voice rose and fell like a siren, grunting like a hungry sow when it dipped too low to actually be a scream, then rising again, shriller and higher.

"Goddamn that hurts my ears," Dale muttered. He pushed his hands down under the waistband of the fatty's shorts and grabbed two handfuls of her butt, squeezing and releasing like bread dough. The fatty continued to hum "The Tennessee Waltz." The freckly one kept her eyes shut. If the redhead was still singing outside, she was being drowned out by the screams in the bedroom. The sweaty man was shouting too. Sometimes the kid knocked on their door at night and Muriel always wanted to let him in. "Everyone's trying to make me deaf!" He pushed the fatty's shorts and underwear down to her knees. She seemed to lose her balance and sat down on her butt, knees apart, looking up at him. But because of the size of her thighs, he could barely see her crack. "Get ready!" he said, shouting above the screams.

"What?"

"Lose the shirt." Dale dropped to his knees between her legs. He started pulling her shirt over her head and at the same time tried to get her legs farther apart by spreading his own knees. It wasn't easy. Her arms were tangled in her sleeves, so Dale left the shirt over the fatty's head and grabbed her giant breasts with both hands. The fatty had to struggle the rest of the way out of her shirt by herself.

"Hey, listen!" she said. The screams went on and on. Then grunting, moaning, and a sound like gargling, and more screams. "'Hey—we're missing it!"

"Wait a sec—you've started something here, you can't just leave." Dale unzipped his pants and pulled himself out. "Come on, come on, we'll hurry." He pushed her to her back.

"Let me help you," the fatty whined.

"I know where it goes." He mounted her and began pumping. She stared up at him, then reached up and cupped his face with both hands and began singing the words to "The Tennessee Waltz." Suddenly the sweaty man started shouting "Here it is, here it is," and the screaming subsided before Dale had come. The fatty kept singing and looking at him, but he went soft, so he abruptly lay down on top of her and made guttural sounds, straining and twitching. Then he sighed, got up, turned around and quickly put himself away. The fatty also jumped to her feet, pulled her pants up, grabbed her shirt and ran down the hall. Dale looked at the freckly one, but she closed her eyes again as soon as he turned toward her. She was swaying slightly from side to side.

"Some party," Dale said.

The sweaty man came out of the hall, drying his face on a towel. "It's all over!"

"You can say that again." Dale checked to make sure his fly was zipped.

"I'm going to ask you nicely to leave," the sweaty man said. He put the towel across the back of his neck and walked once around the room, kicking the pillows back into place, picking up the coffeetable book. He fed the goldfish, glanced once more at Dale, then went back down the hall toward the bedroom. The freckly girl leaped up and ran after him. A baby was crying. Some-one was laughing weakly. Dale started following them down the hall but stopped for a second outside the bathroom. He saw the bucket of slimy blood steaming in the sink.

There was no light in the bedroom. The freckly one and the fatty were kneeling on the bed on either side of the girl, hovering over the plastic bowl and helping to tip it gently, sloshing the water around a baby which was in the bowl.

"What the hell are you doing?" Dale asked.

"I don't want birth to be too traumatic for her," the girl said, "so we're simulating the womb environment and will take her out of it gradually." Her lips looked dark and puffy as though someone had slugged her. But she was smiling. "That's why she's always going to sleep in our bed too," the girl added. The fatty looked up at Dale, wet-eyed and tear-streaked.

"Oh brother," Dale groaned, "don't give me that bullshit." He said it to the fatty, but everyone stared.

"Get the fuck out of here," the young man shouted.

"Danny, the baby—we're supposed to keep our voices smooth and soft for the first several hours."

"Get out, get out!" the young man continued yelling.

"Danny, stop it, please."

"Get out!"

"Danny!" the girl shouted. She picked up her pillow, damp with her sweat, and threw it at Dale. "Get out of here!" Dale swatted the pillow away, then turned and went back into the hall. "Some party," he shouted, but he kept going, out the front door and back down the street toward his own house. By the time he got back to where the sidewalk started, he realized he was humming "The Tennessee Waltz." A coolness had come into the air and splashed over his sweaty face. He entered his front door softly and went over to the couch where the kid slept. The Monopoly game was halfway under the couch and the kid was on his stomach drooling all over his pillow. Dale picked up the game and went back outside. He tried to remember the words to "The Tennessee Waltz" as he walked back to the party. Their door wasn't locked so he went straight in and straight to the bedroom. The baby was nursing on one of the girl's small, pointed breasts. They were *all* on the bed. The redhead had returned and she was on the bed too. Even the man was on the bed, but he jumped off when he saw Dale, and he came toward the door with his fists clenched. When the young man got near enough, Dale thrust the game into his hands.

The young man stared at it.

"What fun!" the girl cried.

Dale watched them make room on the bed and spread the board out, deal the money around, sort through the properties. They covered up a blood spot on the sheet with a dingy white towel. The fatty came around the bed and kneeled with her back to Dale, her heels pushing into her big ass. They were choosing tokens. "I'll take the cannon," the fatty said, then she turned and pointed it at Dale. "Pow pow."

Dale went into the hall and straight to the bathroom. He took the bucket of afterbirth into the backyard and buried it. He didn't want to go home.

## Some Divorces

It's one of those nights when they're together, usually either Monday or Wednesday. Thursday and Saturday evenings Pat teaches swimming at the Y. Tuesday nights she coaches volleyball and Friday she teaches aerobic dance. Sundays she does her work-out at the park and goes to bed early. She's training for her first olympics.

She stopped at the natural food store on her way home from jogging today and bought bulgar wheat. They had tabouli salad for supper, with organic parsley Pat grows in flowerpots. Gene did the dishes while he ate a peanut butter-and-jelly sandwich he fixed himself for dessert. He was making mental calculations for a gadget he hoped to design and build soon: a pedal he could step on to make the back door open automatically when his hands were full. Meanwhile Pat walked to the store to fill her two gallon-bottles with purified low-sodium water. She needs plenty of water for the 24-hour fast which she undergoes once a week to thoroughly clean out her system. The fast started an hour after supper, now into its second hour.

"Okay," Pat says, "let's invite someone over tonight. I feel like having some fun. Who's good?" She sits in a lotus position on the couch.

"Anyone, I guess," says Gene. He glances at the television. He's reading a book which takes place in 2039. He'll only be 92 then. Eating all her health food, he'll probably make it. There's an advertisement on the TV now but a show will start soon.

Pat asks, "What's a four-letter word for nothing?"

"Void. I just read it a page or so ago."

"Does that mean we just had ESP?" She writes it in her crossword puzzle. "Maybe I'll finally finish one of these. So who should we invite over? Who's fun?"

"How about Rick and Sonya. We haven't seen them for a while."

"They can't."

"How do you know?" He turns a page. The lamp is making his neck warm so he turns it off. He needs to design a better lamp that would allow him to sit in his favorite position and still light the page without roasting his neck.

"They've split," Pat says, "and I don't know which one we should still be friends with."

"What happened?"

"Wait, I need a word that means to move about and function almost as though cognizant."

"Try sleepwalk."

"Good. Healthy people don't do that. Anyway, it was strange. Those two did *everything* together. Sonya wouldn't even go out after exercise class because Rick would be picking her up to go do something together. She was putting him through law school—which means she was starting to do pretty well with her singing. Well, so one day he told her he's always liked Mexican women the best. Sonya's Italian. Close but no cigar. So he left."

"Interesting. Is it final?"

"Now it is. He tried to get a percentage of her future earnings and part of the house which she was paying for, but he also wanted a clean record; she said if you try to take *any*thing, the official word will be adultery, so he traded all the property for irreconcilable differences. He got his dog in the settlement."

"I guess he didn't get far enough into law school. Isn't there someone else you could call? Don't we have a lot of other friends?" Gene has a bumper sticker that says *Welcome to California. Now go home.*

Pat searches through a dictionary. "Could you turn the set down—it's so loud."

"That's just the ads. I hate this guy. I hate all guys on beer ads. Such an asshole, and you're supposed to believe if you're an asshole like him and drink their beer, all these girls will fall all over you."

"Maybe the Ballingers could come over. You still see Freddy at the stadium, don't you?"

Gene is a security guard. He wears a red coat, checks people's bags and purses for cans or bottles, looks at tickets, stops people from smoking in the non-smoking sections, stands with his hands behind his back and his back to the action, keeps the crowd off the field after the game. But no one ever tries to get onto the field.

"The Ballingers are ancient history," he says.

"You're kidding. I saw him while I was running yesterday."

"He lives around here." Gene turns the television back up a little. "You think Sonya had a story, listen to this: Freddy moved out because after he asked his wife for sex more than twice a month and she said no, she turned it off completely. Then after six months of nothing, she said if he was having such a hard time living with sex only twice a month, then he probably hadn't been able to survive the past six months with no sex at all, so she charged him with adultery and won. Got the house and kids. Called him a sex maniac in court. They both had good points."

"Wow." She erases a word which was incorrect. "So if that one was supposed to be *cool*, what's this *little quake?*"

"Maybe tremor?"

"You're good at this."

"Yeah, I went to school." Gene went to medical school and finished. He didn't finish his internship. He was a paramedic for a while but didn't like it. He was an orderly but didn't like it either. He tried some hospital administration—an admissions clerk—and hated it. He always knew the people without insurance wouldn't pay, but the doctors made him admit them anyway.

"Well, who else could we invite? I feel good tonight," Pat says. She wets her finger and rubs out another mistake in the puzzle.

"Sissy and Carl live close by." He finishes a chapter, changes his position in the chair, turns the page.

"Wait'll you hear what happened to them!" Pat is putting a small piece of scotch tape on the back side of the puzzle where erasing too many times wore through. "She got a great job in Reno in the orchestra of a show, and she knew she could get another show when that one ended, so she moved there. Carl had a contract to finish up here, then he was going to go to Reno and get a job as a dealer—she had the job all lined up for him. She was in great shape when she left; I saw her a few days before. We had lunch and ran together. That was two months ago. Last month Carl called and told her he wouldn't be coming to Reno because he was living with a woman down the block and helping her raise her five-year-old daughter. Whoops!" Pat has the hiccups.

"Try drinking a glass of water with both lips inside the glass."

"I've already had my quota of water for tonight."

Gene draws in the margins of his book. Whenever there's a description of a machine or tool of the future, he draws it according to the description. Then on his days off he might try to make one or two of them. Several of his gadgets have been patented, but so far he hasn't sold one to a company for production. On his taxes he claims he's self-employed—an inventor—and deducts all the expenses for building the gadgets. He put one of his special can openers that doesn't leave sharp edges on the wall in the kitchen, but Pat doesn't buy canned food because it has added sugar and preservatives.

"Look at that house," Gene says. "No one lives like that. Why don't they show their stuff cleaning a *real* bathroom—look, she's scrubbing a spotless toilet, and the bathroom is as big as the visitors' clubhouse!" His fingers leave damp sweat marks on the book jacket. "Besides, a fool could see the design of that scrub brush is all wrong."

"The weak part breaks it ... what the hell would that be?"

"Chain."

"Of course."

Gene turns several pages in succession. "That story reminds me of Dane Ruggles, only his was even weirder. He had this nice-looking wife. An athlete like you—she ran in races."

"Lots of people run in races without being athletes. Who's Dane Ruggles?"

"A guy I knew. Anyway, listen, he and his wife are both teachers at the university. Once a new teacher came and needed a place to stay for a while until she found something permanent. Get this—she taught human sexuality. Tough grader too. She wasn't as good-looking as Dane's wife, but all the men in the building were dragging their tongues after her. The threesome were all good friends, but, let's see ... I guess the first thing that happened was Dane's wife figured out she wanted to be a lesbian, so she moved out and the new teacher stayed, and pretty soon Dane married *her!*" He turned ten to fifteen pages during the story, blinking once or twice at each.

"I can't get these crazy definitions, *Lee to Grant*, what's this shit!" Pat throws the puzzle down and stands up.

"Probably surrender."

Pat bends at the waist and grabs her ankles, touches her forehead to her knees. Then she spreads her legs, puts both hands flat on the floor between her feet, bends her knees then straightens, stretching the backs of her thighs.

"Well listen to this one," she says, continuing the exercise. "The coach of the men's' track and field team in college—he was on his third wife. They were all runners or gymnasts, but I don't know if they started being athletes after he married them or before. But the third one was doing pretty well, we all heard about her, but he never mentioned her to us, unless we asked, then he would confirm that she had won such-and-such race, but he didn't seem very excited. He had a picture of her on his desk, I think, but we found out they hadn't spoken for a year, maybe more—maybe two years! She would take his phone messages and they had a schedule so one of them was always at home with the kids. Then he started having an affair with one of the girls on our team. She wasn't the best runner. I heard them in the equipment shed. Sometimes at practice he had chalk in his hair. Now how did that work ... oh—something like he and his wife had the divorce papers all ready to sign. As soon as he got the new girl to agree to marry him, his old wife signed, moved out and accelerated her training, and the new wife moved in and handled the old wife's part of the baby-sitting schedule! At least he was careful that last time that he didn't choose one who could ever make it big as a runner." She begins lunging left and right, still bent at the waist, back flat, arms reaching straight on each side.

"Well, hey, I know a pair who did better than that!" He tears a page from his book, leaps out of his chair, turns the television volume up, then stands right in front of the set, the book in one hand, half a page in the other. He'll have to remember that formula he developed for repairing ripped paper without tape.

"This guy I knew at the hospital, he was there as a patient, he had this wife who wanted to be an actress. She drove up to L.A. for lessons, tried out for parts in commercials or walk-on parts in television shows. She was in plays around here, sometimes the lead, but her teacher kept saying she could do better, so she went to New York to train. They didn't have kids and he had his own job, so they were going to endure this temporarily for a while for the sake of her career. They called and wrote letters, but there was no date set for when she would be coming home, and ... wait, get this: it was understood they should each try to get sex somewhere so they wouldn't be climbing the walls. Well, it stretched into *years*. Then he met someone here who he liked so he married her, figuring it had been so long he didn't have a wife anymore, but before he got around to making any divorce final, his first wife came home! Can you imagine it?" Gene is shouting over the television.

Pat begins jogging and punching her hands out in front of herself, to force her heart to send blood to her fingertips at the same time that it is fueling her legs. Her voice comes in puffs of breath. "Hey, wow, that isn't anything like this friend of mine when I was training in Arizona. He was in training too, built *perfect* for the marathon, 5-10, 125 pounds, he's the one who taught me about eating right. Anyway, he had this wife, a slug. She tried to run with us a few times. What an ass she had. Buck teeth, stupid, selfish, the works. And she had this great husband." She increases her pace and punches her hands over her head. "But she used to brag in public about this guy she had on the side whenever she wanted, when she wanted to *eat out*, she said, since she thought her husband had such a strange diet—according to her—just because he wouldn't ingest any animal products, and— and— oh yeah, she used to *ask his permission* before she went to this other guy, like 'may I go have oral sex with so-and-so tonight.'"

The half page Gene was holding is now crumpled into a ball in his fist.

"So anyway," Pat goes on, moving forward slightly so she's jogging on her crossword puzzle. "The guy had taken enough shit and they got a separation and she went home, but they decided to keep in touch and write letters. When he was about to date again, probably ready to ask me out, he wrote to her to tell her not to worry because he was getting over her and he was going to be okay, so she gets scared and writes back that she misses him and wants to try again, so she comes back to him and a week later he catches her at it again! Same guy! I heard he didn't date for five years after his divorce, never won another race, almost joined a monastery, but by that time I'd already left Arizona to come here. The air was too dry there; my sinuses had fits, even though I had a macrobiotic diet."

Another loud advertisement. Gene begins changing channels rapidly and Pat's jogging accelerates. Arms straight, shoulder-level at each side, she raises them over her head and back down, in rhythm with the jogging. Gene spins the channel changer.

"Well, I heard of a guy who was married six times," Gene says. "Not that it's a record, but listen—he married the same two girls three times each. He kept changing his mind. Every time he got divorced, the wife got the house, but since he would always go back with the other, he would just move back into the other house. Essentially he had two houses, two sets of furniture, two sets of kids, etcetera." Each channel has time to bark out a word or half a word before the next cuts it off. "Wait, I've got to remember this right. So he had a pretty good situation, except for the unfortunate time he was hit on the head with ... let's see ... a sledge hammer at work. He forgot which wife he was married to! Forgot which house to go home to. He wandered back and forth between the two of them all night, staring in the windows and—oh yeah!—found out both wives had taken a lover!"

The channel changer breaks off in his hand. He's stuck on a station with no reception. He turns the volume up. The static sounds like a fire. Pat swings into jumping jacks, careful to press both heels to the floor on the extreme part of the jump. Gene swings the antenna in circles.

"That's nothing," Pat gasps. "There was this small town preacher. A *small* town. His wife was the choir. The town doctor was the church elder. He read scriptures before the preacher gave the sermon. The doctor's wife—she took the collection while the preacher's wife sang and the preacher and doctor sat up front bowing their heads."

The next exercise in the routine is circle-jacks, her arms like windmills and her legs doing the same apart-together jumps. Gene drops his book and grabs the antenna with both hands.

"So this preacher," Pat continues, "he gets up one Sunday morning and does his prayer, then the doctor reads from the Bible, then the preacher and his wife sing one of their duets." She catches sweat with her tongue. "So the preacher gets up for the sermon and announces this will be his last week as their preacher. He's going to move to Miami. He's getting a divorce. His wife will stay on as the choir. He's going to marry the doctor's wife. The doctor would be filling in as preacher until they find a replacement. The doctor was marrying the preacher's wife. Then he went on to the sermon of the week!" Her circle-jacks reverse, her arms rotating the other direction.

"I heard one better than *that*." The swinging antenna knocks a glass figure from the bookcase. Pat crushes it under one foot. "Starts with the married couple, right? She thinks something's wrong; she has good reason to be suspicious; he's out most nights. She thinks he's out boozing 'cause he comes in and falls right to sleep. So far not unusual, right? But wait—she follows him one night." The antenna snaps off in his hands. "Let's see ... he stops at about eight houses, but never long enough to do much. He's in and out in fifteen minutes to a half hour—*eight* houses! The wife is thinking, My God, he's insatiable! Then she follows him to the door of the last house and meets him coming out, catches him with the evidence. It was ... a jar of milk! This guy was going around collecting and drinking human milk. It relaxes him, he says. He drinks that last jar on the way home. If she would have a baby, he says, he could drink at home instead of having to go out."

Gene keeps small screwdrivers handy in his pockets. He has blueprints for switch-blade tools so he'll soon be able to keep regular-sized screwdrivers with him. Holding the two pieces of antenna together with one hand, he digs into his pocket with the other. His pants rip.

"I can top that." Each word comes in the rhythm of Pat's circle-jacks.

Gene begins trying to bend the broken pieces of antenna around the stub that's still attached to the TV.

"Listen to this one," Pat says, "it'll kill you. I heard it somewhere. Some religious figure . An elder or officer of some big fundamental church organization. " One arm circles too close to the bookcase. Her hand hits an empty vase. It flies before it falls, breaks only in half, water soaks into the rug. She moves away from the wet spot so she won't slip and strain, pull or sprain anything. She'd forgotten there was water in the vase.

"So he lives half his life—wife, family, eight kids, all go to college, the older ones start to get married, a few grandchildren—then it hits him: he likes boys. More than that, he likes rough boys. Whips, fists, cigarette burns, chains, whatever they can think of, he likes it. That's not all. Wait a sec." She breathes heavily for a moment, head hanging, watching her feet jump out and in. "So here's the story: He shows up at a party wearing leather leggings over tight jeans. Only his butt and crotch stick out of the leather. Metal spikes in a ring around a leather bracelet. Chains around the shoulders of his leather jacket. He comes to the party late but says he's got to leave soon cause the spots get hot and he wants some action."

Tipping the set, Gene works with a screwdriver in back. Pat changes the circle-jacks to jumping-lunges.

"He's got two kids with him—boys—also with leather pants, one has a leather cap, otherwise identical as peas. My sons, he says. It's father-and-son night. It ends up— It ends up— He blows his house up. An accident. Had the oven open, gas on, flame lit, pulled his pants down, stuck his butt in."

The screwdriver hits a nerve and the set spits sparks from the back. The static stops. The screen pops, cracks. Luckily it was a rubber-handled screwdriver.

"He just wanted to get a little singed on his backside, to spice up any action he found that night. But he farted. Boom! Human torch. Running down the street. The leather melted and fused to his body. His famous last words: No one could ever experience anything more exciting than *that!*"

"Well!"

Pat stops jumping. Gene turns away from the set. She looks at him; he looks at her. His eyes are sleepy and brown, hers wide and hazel.

Gene sits down without his book. Pat does her warm-down. Feet shoulder-width apart, bending at the waist, back flat, head to her right knee. She runs her hands up and down the taut back of her leg, thigh to calf. Then with hands on both ankles, head to the floor between her legs, pressing gently but firmly. Next, head to her left knee, pressing, feeling the warm elastic length of her muscles. She walks her hands out in front of her feet, careful to keep her heels down and legs straight, back flat, presses her chest to the floor. Sweat runs from her face and neck and drips from her chin to the rug. Standing again, she takes five slow breaths, swinging her arms up to expand her ribcage and allow the maximum amount of oxygen. Her shirt sticks to her body. Her underwear is soaked. She inhales the pure and earthy smell of herself.

In the bathroom she lets the water run, waiting for it to get hot. Arms crossed over her chest, she squeezes her biceps, massages her neck and shoulders. She looks in the mirror. She's 31. The olympic trials start next year.

She washes her face first, using organic apricot soap with bits of crushed apricot seed, then with cream of aloe vera. Washes her arms, shoulders and chest with pure jojoba soap, then applies cream of mineral oil and unprocessed bee pollen to her face, neck and shoulders. She doesn't use deodorant because it blocks the pores and doesn't allow poisons to leave the body. Her toothpaste is made of sea kelp.

She comes back into the living room holding a creamcolored towel over her breasts. "I guess it's too late to invite anyone over now." She uses one end of the towel to dry her hair. "I guess we could go to bed."

"That's true." He holds a beer in both hands in his lap.

She turns on his reading lamp, adjusts it over his shoulder, picks up her crossword puzzle and goes into the bedroom.

# The Statue Maker

It's more a story about him than me. And he wasn't crazy. He was sad—sadder than any sad person I've ever known before or since; profoundly sad, abjectly sad, abstractly sad. That kind of sadness gives you some kind of weird energy, makes you hideously attractive and deliciously repulsive at the same time. But he was still more attractive than repulsive. I don't know why. For example, the acne scars on his cheeks—in the middle of all that mess, he had dimples.

I do look for jobs, but it's probably not even a job that I want. I want to be able to make a move without wondering what it means and how he'll react, how it'll make him change—from child to brute, from lout to gentleman, from grinning fool to leering asshole, from the hard and scaley businessman bachelor back into the vulnerable adolescent he must've been at fifteen when he left home. But he wasn't crazy! I heard him carry on intelligent conversations behind his office door. He put in volunteer hours in a runaway hotline center. He was on the board of directors of the symphony and opera. His investment company was not in a state of collapse but getting stronger every day. He was the local fancy skateboard champion and won the city-wide tango competition every year. Everyone wants to just say he was crazy and I should forget about it. Has anyone ever really tried to forget something that everyone's telling them to forget?

I wish all this could be condensed enough to fit on the three-inch line they put on applications to explain "reason for leaving your last job." I tried several shortened versions: Because I talked in my sleep. Because I didn't talk in my sleep (but he wanted me to). Couldn't concentrate with him around. Concentrated too much with him around. Because I didn't know what he wanted, he never gave a title to my position. Or because of an unfortunate party to which I was not invited, but taken. A million excuses, no real reasons. I leave that line blank now.

The party is still a bit of a mystery. Who planned it? Who paid the caterer? Why didn't I hear about it until the last minute when they surrounded my desk, helped me into my sweater, put my purse over my arm, closed my appointment book ...? Aren't you coming to the party, Deanne? You have to!

For what, I asked, what occasion?

Someone said maybe it was my farewell party (if we're lucky).

I was blindfolded so as not to spoil the surprise. After a cab ride—which I think I paid for—and being led by both hands for about a block, surrounded by their giggles, we went up an elevator, down a hall, and ended up in a hotel suite. By the time my blindfold was removed, they'd all put on masks, like outlaw bandanas. There was a portable stereo blaring out lyricless tango music. Then they held me down, a funnel in my mouth—I had to swallow or drown. It was so uncharacteristic of my co-workers to behave that way. The last party they'd had was cookies and coffee in the rec room during the lunch hour. And, as bad as this sounds, next thing I knew I was asleep, back at my desk at eight in the morning when Davis arrived and woke me, sniffing the air like a hound. "You're a little disheveled this morning. And what's that smell?"

"Was I here all night?"

"I don't know, were you?"

"You would know," I said. "Was I home last night? Wasn't I sleeping on the couch as usual?"

"Actually, I didn't check. Come to think of it, though, I didn't hear anyone talking in their sleep. Too bad. Maria would've been amused."

"I'm not drunk, not anymore. Am I? I mean, how long is it supposed to last?" I hadn't even looked at him yet, except his feet—I could see that much, his sneakers.

"I never told you," he said, laughing, "last week, I guess it was Sue—she thought you were hilarious. Really, you were great. We must've sat there beside the couch for twenty minutes listening to you. Of course I had to prompt you a little, to keep you going."

"Weren't you at that party? I thought I saw you—"

"How would you possibly remember? But, oh boy, that night last week, you said something like 'I can't even hear you anymore.' Sue was cracking up. No, that's right, it was Sara. I said, 'I'm shouting in your ear.' You said, 'But your hands are so fast.' Then you got mad at us for laughing. I thought for sure you were awake, the way you tried to kill Sara. Don't you remember? I doubt she'll ever come back, but that's okay. It was worth it."

"It's okay? You're not going to fire me?"

"Oh that. Yes, you're history around here. Start packing, baby."

"It was a conspiracy!"

"Think so? How's it feel?" He was wearing jeans, a pink dress shirt and red tie. I'd finally managed to look up at him. I knew I stunk from more than just booze that had sloshed out of the funnel—if there had been a funnel, if there had been a party. The memory was already fading. My hair was literally matted. I was feeling the back of it, half expecting something to move. For some reason my eyes were fixed on his tie—it was a narrow tie, my eyes felt crossed from staring at it. He'd worn that same tie when he'd asked me to share his apartment, and every time he wore it after that I'd had to smile and was in a good mood all day, until I went home and remembered I was still sleeping on the couch. My back would ache in the mornings, and sometimes I had to get up early to do stretching exercises and a girl would come sneaking out of his bedroom at six or six-thirty. Usually the girl would get mad and leave in a huff because I was supposed to stay on the couch with the blanket over my head until the coast was clear. If his night had gone well, he might be angry at me for getting up early, but if the visitor had bombed, he wouldn't say anything one way or the other.

Even before I moved into his apartment, I was always aware of him, like an electrical excitement that remained hovering, waiting to cause lightning, and he might at any moment burst out of his office to pace around the main room, picking up objects from people's desks, putting them down on other desks, sometimes carrying a stapler and vase of flowers halfway around the room until something else caught his eye. He was always moving. Even when he talked to one person at a time, like at my interview, he sat, then stood, then walked around his desk, pausing behind me to put his hands on the back of my chair and rock it a few times, then jumping up to hit the ceiling with his hand. He offered me donuts and coffee which he didn't have. I accepted, then looked around for the coffeepot, saw none, but he never brought it up again. He was too interested in where I came from. "You were born in Idaho!" He jumped from his seat again. "Yes, but—"

"Great state, isn't it, nice summer evenings for playing outside."

I shrugged. "It's the kind of state no one ever thinks about."

"I do. A lot." He picked up my application, seemed to read it, then folded it in half, and the half in halves. "I was born there too, did you know that?"

"No," I smiled.

"I mean, could you tell? Is there anything similar about the two of us, anything you recognize?"

"Actually, we seem to be fairly different," I laughed. I was about ten to fifteen pounds overweight, sitting there calmly, quite comfortable, just the usual job-interview jitters. He was thin and continued moving around the room, coming back now and then to fold my application another time.

"You're right about that, sister. I mean, remember that, Miss ...."

"Bacilla."

"You married? Where'd you get a name like that?"

"No, not married. Engaged though."

"I'm going to hire you," he said, "know why? I don't even know yet myself, but there is a reason. You'll find out. Maybe you'll even be sorry. That'd be nice. You'd deserve that, wouldn't you?" He was smiling, showing almost all his teeth, his eyebrows raised and brow creased many times.

I laughed. It was that point in an interview when the tension would be dissipating.

"I'm serious," he said, the same smile, but his eyebrows came down.

"Of course you are!" I chuckled. "Why else would anyone want a job, except to be sorry they got it!"

"No, I'm serious." His smile eased but didn't disappear. He was pinching his thumb in a staple-remover. "Have a family? Bet they're all waiting by the phone up in Idaho to find out how their little Precious makes out with her first job in the big city, but you won't call, will you— no, you'll wait until they call you. Want to know why no one called me when I arrived from Idaho? They didn't know I was here. Bet they don't even know now. Do they?" Abruptly he sent me out of his office.

Later that same day there was a birthday party in the lobby. Someone handed him a piece of cake, but he just held it, drawing in the frosting with his finger, but never ate any. "I'm fasting," he said, "cleansing myself." Every time I took a bite of cake, I looked up to find him staring at me, grinning. When he asked me to move in with him, I didn't have to hesitate for a second before I agreed.


After I was fired, I went home and found he'd moved out. The apartment was completely bare, except for my clothes in a pile on the closet floor. He'd taken all the hangers. My head ached so badly that I couldn't cry. I took a bath and dried myself with toilet paper, then sat on the living room floor where we'd played Statue-Maker the first night I lived there. We would've had more room for Statue-Maker without the furniture. I'd bruised both my shins against the T.V. table and skinned my knuckles on the furnace grate, bumped my head on the coffee table. He hadn't even told me the rules first, just grabbed my arm, twirled me around and around, then let go so I spun and staggered and fell, then he shouted "Freeze! No, wait, you can't move, didn't they teach you the rules? Okay we'll have to do that one over." He had to explain the game which, originally, was only played on the lawn on summer evenings after supper or at family gatherings. They picked the statue maker who spun the others one at a time, let go, shouted "Freeze," and the statue was formed. Then one by one he titled them. When he pressed a secret button, they had to act out whatever title they'd received from the statuemaker. Sometimes, he claimed, there were fifteen statues all acting out parts at the same time.

"Did you have a big family?" I asked.

"Not anymore." He didn't spin me again like he'd said he was going to. He turned his back and went into his bedroom, saying over his shoulder, "I ever tell you about my grandmother? I will someday." Then he closed the bedroom door.

I waited several hours for him to come back out, finally falling asleep on the couch. The next night he gave me sheets and a pillow and apologized because it wasn't a fold-out sofa-bed.

One night that first week, I stopped at a grocery store on the way home from work. There hadn't been any food in the house since I'd moved in, not a shred. I still got home before him, as usual. When he arrived, at quarter to ten, the roast was well-done and the mashed potatoes were hardening. "That's okay," he said, "I'm fasting. I would've hired a cook if that's what I wanted. Wouldn't've even gotten home *this* soon, except I wasn't lucky, know what I mean? A peck at the doorway, then goodnight, *slam*, flip the lock and slide the chain across."

"You had a *date*?" I could speak but couldn't move. I was standing in the kitchen with a cooking spoon in one hand, but my fingers couldn't manage to stay holding on. The spoon fell and bits of potato spattered on the floor. A slow smile crept onto his face the way a candle flame becomes a wildfire—not noticeable at first because it doesn't seem dangerous.

"Doesn't that seem a bit ... unusual?" I finally asked.

"How so? You mean because I didn't get anywhere with her? Que será será."

"I mean, what about me?"

"Is that all you think about?" He paused, then sneered and added, "Still?"

"Well ... we live together ...."

The sneer was already gone. "Hey, yeah, what about that! This's great. See, I spend a lotta time thinking about ways to avoid all the puppy love or adolescent crushes or any of the thousands of bad reasons the girls in the building have for hitting on the guys. But, hey, I just realized I can put you to good use, can't I? Yeah, great idea—from now on, as far as they're concerned, I'm taken, right? So it's hands-off or the boss's secretary'll whomp them!"

"I'm not your secretary."

"Okay okay. Hey, you're free to do whatever, you know, as long as no one sees you. Know what I mean? Sure, fine, have an illicit affair behind my back, but I don't want some lovesick typist trying to make points by telling me she saw you—"

"I don't want to see anyone else."

"Good, that's even better. That's perfect. 'Night."

I was still standing in the kitchen. The house went dark, except the light over the sink. From there I could see the sofa and my sheets, folded as I'd left them that morning. It took a long time before I was able to go into the living room and lie down. On the coffee table there was a letter, ready to mail, to my fiancé, breaking it all off. It was still there when I opened my eyes in the morning. I'd barely moved in my sleep, the sheet was still neatly spread over me. I lay there even after he came into the living room in his underwear, brushing his teeth, and watched some of a morning cartoon show. His gaunt, lined face added five years to his age—which was somewhere in his late 30's, nearing 40—but his body, from the neck down, was no more than sixteen. He grinned at me with the toothbrush making a bulge in one cheek where the acne scars were. On my way to work, I went ahead and mailed the letter.

How could I regret it? That same evening he arrived home early and came straight into the kitchen where I was preparing one portion of canned tomato soup. He turned the burner off and led me by the hand to the sofa, and we sat right on top of my pillows and blankets, like lying on a mattress that's too soft so it billows up around you. His eyes were intense but not frightening, as though they could glow in the dark in an abandoned house and be welcoming, instead of blood-curdling. And he kissed me without greediness, without urgency, as though simultaneously drawing me gently into his mouth and pouring himself slowly into mine.

Then he said, "I've owed you that for a long *looong* time."

Yet I continued spending my nights on the narrow couch. Sleeping there without moving wasn't difficult, even though I woke often—I just lay there without bothering to move until I slept again. The apartment made muffled sounds like cats in an attic even if Davis hadn't come home yet. But if I was dreaming of a howling wind or screaming storm, the shriek ended abruptly when I rose to the surface and woke. I never knew what woke me up. Sometimes I just knew I was going to wake up before I actually did. And once I was awakened by a hot feeling of joy and found Davis crouched beside the couch, watching me. He giggled when I opened my eyes. His hair was wet and looked sticky, smelled awful, but not a familiar odor. His mouth looked dark and his eyes like two black holes. I whispered, "Davis, are you okay?"

"What?" He giggled again. "Know what you said this time? Incredible. You said, 'They're bowling and wrestling with their dog.' Remember saying that? What were you talking about?"

"Davis, I don't talk in my sleep."

"How do you know?"

"I would hear it and wake up," I said. "Let me help you back to bed."

"Knock it off." He was surly for a moment, then giggled again. I reached to touch his hair, but he jerked his head back, laughing in a falsetto.

"You don't even know," he said. "You probably don't even know that I recognized you right away— marching into my office with an immaculate application, well-scrubbed, smelling great, soft and pudgy. You think I can't spot someone who was always kept well-fed and comfortable, catered to and admired, everyone took turns burping you and you never wore a dirty playsuit or bib—and haven't you turned out just the way I would've expected."

"Davis?"

"Get your hands off me!"

"You better go to bed."

"Oh *good*, I like the way you've learned to be so concerned about *me*. For a while I thought you were hopeless, like pushing you out of a window was my only solution. Did you know that's what I was thinking of doing during your interview, when I was asking What's the primary quality of an office manager? You think I ask questions like that 'cause I need to know? I never even had that position available, I made it up, right then, a nice generic title. And I gagged on your answer ... I can still quote it in my sleep: To make sure above all else I always deserve the respect or even friendship of the other employees. It wasn't the answer that was so ironic, it was you saying it. I could've cut your tongue out on the spot but went ahead and hired you. What the goddamn hell for? Not a plan in my head, I swear, I saw you and almost panicked, but it's really worked itself out: I think you're losing weight. And do I detect some pimples on your forehead? You're biting your nails, aren't you? Where's your expensive-but-tasteful engagement ring?"

"I told you I broke it off."

"That's so perfect!"

"Davis, I really do want to talk about this. I think we need to get some things into the open. But you're in no condition—"

"I'm fine," he snapped.

"Okay, but before we talk, you need to think. Ask yourself why you wanted me to live here. Was it just to help you pay the rent?"

"Good, you noticed I was deducting it from your salary. Why didn't you say anything."

"I didn't mind."

"God, I'm a genius." Suddenly he rested his forehead against the edge of the couch. I got up, took his arm and led him back to his room. He wasn't dressed. My hand was resting lightly on his side and I could feel his ribs sharply underneath his skin. He pulled away from me, turned on his bedroom light and sat down on the bed beside a girl who was sleeping there. I could only stand and stare. Then I heard Davis chuckling. "It's so perfect, I must have remarkable intuition. It's priceless. Oh, sorry, forgot my manners. Deanne, this is Cristy." The girl didn't wake up. There was a tequila bottle beside her, peeking out from under the sheet. "That name remind you of anything?" he said.

I was motionless, but my voice found a way out. "Christmas?"

"No, idiot, christening. Weren't you ever baptized? Course you were."

"I don't remember."

"What? Not to remember the big day!" He got up and moved toward me. "Like a goddamn coming-out party for a drooling baby. You lie there and wet your pants over and over while everyone kills each other trying to get a look at you or bring you cake or feed you your first glob of ice cream, and some people get completely forgotten and could starve to death for all you care."

I was standing with my arms folded and shoulders hunched. "I can't figure out if you're talking about real babies or debutantes—"

"I'm talking about you!" He hit me with a backhanded swing, knocking me down and out the door at the same time.

On the bare kitchen counter, I found an envelope containing my old resumé and a new letter of recommendation, this one from Davis. On the envelope he'd written, "It shouldn't be too hard to get another job, now that you've had all this valuable experience. Ha ha. See you around, party-girl!" He'd also enclosed a list of job openings. I wasn't drunk anymore, it couldn't't've lasted that long—I recognized the last one on the list was *my* job—what had been my job yesterday—but still no real position title given, just "help wanted" and an address.

It didn't matter if it was August or January, every office lobby was kept too cold. One after another, I sat there and rubbed my chilly arms, trying to keep the hair from standing on end, until someone poked a head through the inner door and told me to go ahead and leave. Once, as I waited, the inner door was left open, and I saw a man reading my letter of recommendation from Davis. I was positive I saw the man light a candle then hold the letter over the flame until a message written in lemon juice between the lines became visible. The man looked up at me while he lowered the letter onto the flame and let it catch fire, then dropped the burning paper into a large glass ashtray. But when the receptionist told me to leave, she handed me my resumé and the letter, still clean and white. I stood there stupidly staring at it, rubbing my thumb over the printed lines until the paper was smudged and unusable. The receptionist said, "Go on, you're free to go. Good luck." Maybe it was my imagination—I thought she added, as she was sliding her glass window closed, "Hurry now, Davis is expecting you."

It wouldn't be like begging for my old job back, to go back to him and reapply—as though I'd been on an extended leave or sabbatical and was returning, or as though I'd never been there in the first place. His letter of recommendation called me gifted and confident, difficult to discourage or depress, a born winner. Wouldn't a person like that be expected to return?

The cold lobby and vinyl seats seemed all too familiar, except maybe even colder. I'd worn a sweater this time, but my legs were pocked with goosebumps; my toes, fingers and nose were numb. I doubled over in my chair, pressing my chest to my knees, hugging my shins. A voice over an intercom told the receptionist to send in the next one, even though I was the only one there and had been the only one there for over an hour. I went through the inner door and sat in a chair, hands pressed together between my knees, eyes focused on my thumbs, trying to control my shivering by hunching my shoulders and pulling my neck in. The trouble was, the person that he'd described in the recommendation hadn't come back—I had.

"Idaho!" he exclaimed. "You come from Idaho too, how about that! Say, what did you like to do on summer evenings after supper?"

I knew I had to look at him, but couldn't seem to move my neck. In the ticking silence, I could picture how he was grinning, showing teeth, but my eyes were shut.

Finally, when I knew I'd raised my head, I opened my eyes and tried to look at him as though I only vaguely recognized him. "Have I already applied here?" I said. "Have I tried here before?"

"We won't talk about the last person who held this job."

"That's fine with me," I said, and actually felt a sigh of relief.

"You wouldn't believe it, though," he said, "the way she acted, stepped all over people, especially her family, know what I mean? And after what happened to her great-grandmother ...."

"I didn't ever have a great-grandmother. I mean, not living."

"You're wrong," he said, "but I'm going to stay calm." He was standing, leaning forward with his palms on the bare desktop. There wasn't anything on the desk but his hands. "Naturally I expected you to say something like that, you wouldn't've even known she was alive."

"I'm going to go now," I said, which actually surprised me, and I didn't move.

"Please, wait ...." His hands were still resting on the desk, though he had lowered himself back into his chair. He wasn't even drumming his fingers. He wasn't flipping his tie or unscrewing a pen or taking staples out of a stapler and picking them apart until he had a pile of loose, individual staples. "Maybe you'll be interested to know that I was perfectly okay until I saw you," he said. "I mean that. Then, seeing you ... and how you obviously had no shame or regret, no feelings whatsoever ... I've heard of babies being dropped like a bomb, but you took the cake ... both literally and figuratively, I guess—

they must've crammed over half that cake into your mouth ... and from the looks of you when you first walked in here, nothing had changed."

"I was a little overweight, but—"

"What I want to know," he said, "is how can *any* baby be the cutest baby anyone's ever seen?"

"I don't think too much about babies, to tell the truth."

"You think you were the last baby ever born? I've got news for you—"

"Davis," I said. "I'm only going along with this because I had to come back and see you. Okay, you don't have to give me my job back—or any job—but, please, come back to the apartment, I—"

"That's disgusting."

My chilliness went beyond shivering, and I sat like a stone. He'd recently had a haircut and was wearing a new light blue sports shirt and black silk tie, loosened a little to allow the shirt to be open at the collar so I could see the soft spot on his neck that moved up and down when he spoke. "I always wanted to talk to you about Idaho," he said. "What's it like now?"

"I was born there by mistake. My parents were on vacation—"

"Liar."

"It's the truth. My mother was one of those fat women who didn't even know she was pregnant." My voice sounded numb and wooden and brittle, but if I could've cried, I might've gotten a little warmer.

"Don't you think I should be able to remember perfectly well?" he said. "We all lived in Idaho. There were five children in my father's family—he was the youngest and I was his youngest—so you can imagine how many cousins I had. Then one of them had a baby. And the whole thing fell apart after that."

"Davis, if you'd like, I'll help you find your family."

"Oh, right. After I left they probably wanted to pretend I never existed. And the feeling was mutual. Until you showed up here. You always have a way of showing up, don't you. Just like you did then, dropped like a bomb. Well, you know what? When you showed up at your cristening party, everyone stopped everything. They spent the rest of the day stuffing you with food, snapping pictures, passing you around. You know where Nana was? In her room. They forgot to go get her and bring her out to the party. You wouldn't've cared—she was my grandmother, not yours."

I had a pounding sinus headache from the air conditioner, like the cold had frozen the front part of my brain. I couldn't keep my eyes open and recalled if you fall asleep in freezing weather, you'll most likely freeze to death. But I couldn't even move my hands to make my fingers prop my eyelids open.

"But God," he said, "when you read about it in the newspaper, you wonder how people can kill babies. But I would've taken you by the arm, whipped you around over my head and let you fly, put you into orbit if I could've. That's what I should've done. You changed everything. We hadn't gotten together for three or four years before that party, and the last time, when they'd called us all inside from playing after supper, it was my turn to be the statue maker. But it turned out there was no next time." He pounded a fist on the desk, startling me enough to get my eyes open. He had crawled up onto the desktop and was crouched there on all fours in front of me, his face just inches away, his eyes very shiny, his lashes wet, his nose reddened and running a little, his teeth biting down on his lower lip. "Maybe that christening party or coming-out party—no, I'll call it a popping out party, a bomb-dropping party—maybe they told you about it or showed you pictures of yourself with frosting all over your fat laughing face .... It was pitiful, sickening. They stood around like adults and talked about sprinkling systems and antiques and babies. Why shouldn't I just get out of there, I bet they never even tried to find me, did they? Didn't they ever say, Long ago you had this uncle, really just a boy last time we saw him .... Didn't they say anything?"

"My mother came from Colorado," I whispered. "Please stop this, Davis ...."

"Don't touch me!" He backed up, practically slid off the desk and back into his chair. My hands were still pressed between my knees. My breath was shallow and quick because there was a sharp pain in my chest if I breathed deep, as though I'd been swimming for a long time in very cold water. As I stared at him, his face twisted and his body began to jerk. He stood and sort of staggered around the desk, practically collapsed beside me on the floor, his head in my lap. "They were just too preoccupied with the damn baby to remember that she was still in her room, but I knew." His hands were clutching fistfuls of my dress. "I knew she was in there, I thought about her. I could've gone in there and brought her out or even stayed in there with her, I could've brought her a piece of cake, but it was my turn to be the statue maker, I had to be ready. Any minute they might've gone outside to play—"

There was a warm wet spot on my dress where his mouth was. But when he lifted his head and the air conditioning hit the spot, my teeth chattered. Otherwise, besides that, I didn't move. He backed up until he hit the desk, boosted himself up and sat on the desktop, then swung his legs around so his back was to me. "Okay," he said. "That's all. Now if you want to go on with your life like a normal person, it's okay with me."

But I didn't move for a long time, even after he left the room.

# Happy Story

Abigail is vomiting over having to take her mother to the party.

"I never once complained," Mrs. Cheever says, rapping on the bathroom door with her cane. "Every time your speech team went out of town to compete, I was there helping."

Abigail sobs into the toilet.

It's Abigail's old speech teacher, the team coach, having a birthday party: forty years old. She hasn't seen him in nine years. She also hasn't said much (if anything) since she gave her last speech: catching his eye, then stopping in the middle, a sentence dangling, "...the important point to remember is—" Nine years ago.

With her cane, Mrs. Cheever pushes the bathroom door open and brings her wheelchair into the doorway. Abby squats, her chin on her knees, hugs her shins. Wisps of her hair are wet, sticky, hanging near her oversized black eyes.

"Abby, all our friends will be there, you'll see." She leans forward and pinches Abby's throat with thumb and index finger. "Say you'll go. What could be more important to you than your old mother wanting to go to a party?"


Arriving at the party, entering the garden patio through sliding glass doors, Mrs. Cheever hoots and laughs, "Whee!" She waves her cane in the air, circling their heads. Abby ducks. She pushes her mother to the gift table where Mrs. Cheever stands to kiss the balmy face of Darrell White. Abby helps her mother to sit again; she removes the wrapped box from Mrs. Cheever's lap, adds it to the mountain of gifts. Darrell is watching this too solemnly, considering the occasion. Then he remembers to smile happily as guests greet him. He is standing in front of Mrs. Cheever. She holds his hips, one in each hand, talks toward his loins, "Forty years old and still slim as a boy." She pokes his belly, looks up and laughs, mouth wide. Abby looks down her mother's throat.

Several lumpy women have pulled their lawn chairs close to Darrell, but none closer than Abby's mother. She takes a piece of twine and ties his chair to the arm of her wheelchair. Darrell looks at Abby with wet brown eyes. The lawn chairs form a circle. Abby is on the outside, the backs of several wispy heads in front of her. One is her own mother. Mrs. Cheever suggests a game: "We've got a circle here, how about spin the bottle!"

Abby tries to fasten her mother's top button and fix her collar, but Mrs. Cheever swats her hands away.

"Loan me a cig, Darrell," Mrs. Cheever pleads. "Remember how I use-ta bum them off you? Remember?"

Abby takes her mother's cigarette and crumples it. Mrs. Cheever scratches the back of Abby's hand with her fingernails until Abby opens her fist and lets her mother have the pieces of paper and balled-up tobacco. Mrs. Cheever smokes happily. "We tried to quit together, Darrell, remember? On that trip to Pasadena, you and I on the bus, we wanted a smoke so *badly*. We were so nervous, remember? The biggest competition of the year. In order to help ourselves quit, we promised to smoke only if we *didn't* win, remember? And we won! State champions!"

He listens to her, nodding vaguely, glancing around, remembering to smile. Japanese lanterns hang from the patio beams. The fly paper buzzes. Darrell says something. Abby only hears the soft smile without words. He lifts his chin and scans the crowd, shuts his eyes once slowly. Then resumes the party smile.

Someone behind Abby says, "I'm happy to see someone else my age showed up." He is very tall, too tall. "I'll bet you're an ex-team member." He folds his arms across his chest. "I'm Guy, the other speech coach."

Mrs. Cheever's laugh is honking. She raps the table leg with her cane, kicking her heels against cross poles on her chair. She bounces in her seat. "That's good, oh, that's a good one. I heard one the other day, listen, Darrell, over here: a coupla girls were at a bar...."

"Sick, isn't it," Guy says.

Abby sips wine, watches red creep up the back of her mother's neck.

"Yeah, sick," Guy agrees with himself. "But lookit them."

The guests lean forward in their chairs toward Darrell. Their eyes sparkle at him. There is no one forgotten or tired. Especially not Mrs. Cheever as, with happy giggling, she delivers her punch-line. The rest wait for Darrell's bland smile. They lap it up. The party is filled with subtle eagerness, almost like the sound of them gobbling the processed buffet food.

"How's the team look this year, Darrell?"

"We gonna win the state?"

"We got any debaters, or all comics?"

"Never fails, everyone wants to be a comic."

"Good evening ladies and germs."

"How we gonna get those kids to settle down?"

Darrell's head slowly pivots as though by motor, passing his smile out to the guests. Everyone is ignited. Darrell makes sure he gives at least a word to each of them. Abby sees his mouth move, but no sound. The party guests feast. Darrell takes a second to glance quickly at Abigail. She keeps her hands gently on the back of her mother's wheelchair, her chin lifted, her eyelids lowered.

"You know," Guy says. "Not a single team member here. We invited them. Not one showed." He puts his hands in his pockets and stands on his toes. Abby's head reaches to the middle of his chest. "You take care of your mother, huh? Full time work? Well, I was thinking...." He comes down from tip-toe and taps her shoulder to make her stop staring at his second shirt button. "Maybe we could go out, catch a movie—hey, one of those funky surrealist plays is in town, maybe you and I ...?"

Abby lifts her chin slowly and lets the Japanese lanterns bob in her eyes. Wine color springs to her cheeks, her lips part, perhaps a smile, she's going to answer, to actually speak.

Taking a straw and careful aim, Mrs. Cheever shoots a mouthful of punch onto the back of Abby's neck. Abby leaps to attention as the mouthful runs down her spine, into her underwear and a little dribbles down her legs.

"Pay attention," her mother says. "I *said* I hafta go to the toilet."

Darrell stands to get more beer. Mrs. Cheever lunges forward in her chair, grabbing for his arm. "Stay with me. Do I hafta get my handcuffs out?" Abby pulls her mother back. Mrs. Cheever waits until Abby puts her cup to her lips, then pokes her cane into Abby's stomach.

Down on hands and knees, Abby chokes. Darrell reaches behind Mrs. Cheever to pat Abigail's back. She hacks and spits up wine. It runs down her chin. He tries to lift her face, but she drools on his hand.

"This is an important moment," the hostess announces. "We want to preserve it. The video camera is running over here. Everyone be sure to get into the picture. We'll play it back later. Come and give your best wishes to Darrell into the microphone."

They escort Darrell to a position in front of the lens and pose for group shots, clinging to each other for balance while trying to squeeze everyone into the picture, a bouquet of smiling heads. Darrell's tranquil voice is killed by their shrill gaiety. He grins, then rubs his eyes. The smoke is thick. He clears the air with one hand. Smiles.

"Abigail, get me over to the camera with Darrell," Mrs. Cheever says. Abby is sitting flat on her ass. "C'mon, Abby, this is *important*." Abby stands, clutches the back of a chair for balance, catches her breath. "I can't wait for you all night." Mrs. Cheever pushes Abigail into the pool in order to get past her. The cameraman turns the lens toward the splash. "You think *that* was a splash ...," Mrs. Cheever says. She throws a cement cinder block from the garden into the pool after Abby. "Hope she can catch!"

"Time for cake and presents!" the hostess calls. The frosting is blue and gold. School colors. A shaky blue script says, "It's important to stand up, put your chest out and speak as though you're *right*."

"The motto! The motto!" Mrs. Cheever leads the laughter. "Get this on film, our team motto."

"Stupidest motto I've ever heard." Guy squats by the edge of the pool. Abby lifts the cinder block to the deck then slithers out of the water. Staring at the brick, he adds, "Maybe we'd better forget about the play."

She silently spits water and creeps under a chair. The camera and spotlight are still on her. Guy takes a piece of cake and smashes it into the camera lens.

Most of the guests are horrified and stand facing Guy. Mrs. Cheever grabs a plastic knife and points it at him. Darrell is tall and grins—desperately—his mouth taut, teeth showing, his eyes mostly white. The guests hesitate, then turn back toward Darrell. His face relaxes. He rubs his eyes again, one at a time, with a single finger. Finally his smile once again joins the Japanese lanterns bobbing gently, glowing warmly.

"Were you *really* surprised?" the hostess asks. Everyone eats cake. Abby's mother spits out the raisins.

"Time for presents!"

The pile of packages is actually taller than Darrell. Abby can see his lips move as he reads cards. The cameraman's spotlight does finally go off. The lanterns are still like magic.

Mrs. Cheever is maneuvering her chair by herself, knocking over tables and chairs as she hurries back to Darrell's side. "Open mine first—it's important."

He is already the tallest; still, Guy stands on a picnic bench. Mrs.Cheever has locked her wheels into place beside Darrell, pats his butt and reaches under the gift table with her cane to knock Abby on the head. "Come *here*," she says in a spitty whisper. Abby crawls under the table, past Darrell's shoes, behind her mother's chair, and stands up, resuming her position. Darrell is fighting with a ribbon on a package. "Gimme that," Mrs. Cheever says. She bites the ribbon in half. "See, this is from me," Mrs. Cheever gurgles, holding up a very pink T-shirt in front of her own huge chest. "Think of me when you wear it."

The pink T-shirt says, "Think Of Me." Mrs. Cheever is pulling it over Darrell's head. She smoothes it down over his sweater, then she roars laughter, mouth open, spraying cake.

Abby's tears drip into her mother's dyed-red hair. "You're such a kill-joy," Mrs. Cheever says and sticks a finger into each of Abby's eyes, then returns to the party.

Trying to pull Abby's hands away from her face, Darrell holds one of her wrists for a second, but someone thrusts another gift into his arms. He rips the paper hastily.

The hostess is standing with Mrs. White, Darrell's tall wife, on the outside of the circle of chairs. "He is surprised," the hostess says.

"Yes, I think so," Mrs. White answers. "I'm so happy we did this."

The hostess claps her hands. "Everyone, please listen. This is a good time to hold our first parents club meeting for this year's speech team. You older parents are invited to join us again, we have some important decisions to make."

Everyone sits in the circle. Darrell needs a place to sit. "Here," screams Mrs. Cheever, patting her lap.

"First of all, what should we wear to the competition trips this year? We ought to have some sort of uniform so people know who we are. It's pretty important."

"White blouses."

"I'm not buying a blouse. T-shirts are cheaper," says a whale of a lady. "And more comfortable."

"They're ugly, especially on you," Mrs. Cheever says.

"Let's remember priorities."

"It's important to have a good discipline policy."

"It's always been too soft. Sometimes I feel like smacking faces."

Finally Abby finishes rubbing her eyes. She removes her fists from her sockets. On her mother's lap, Darrell is turned away from the meeting, smileless, looking backwards at Abby. She shuts her eyes again. An ordinary man says, "What do you think, Darrell?" Abby can't hear his answer. She does hear soft laughter.

"What about lunch," says the big lady. "Do we eat with the kids, before or after?"

"No, it's more important to decide where we can smoke."

Some women laugh. Tinkling chimes are hanging with the Japanese lanterns.

"We'd better talk about what's important," the hostess says. Some women are still laughing.

"And that's helping the school to win," the ordinary man says.

"The turnstile turners are joining the team," Guy remarks. He is very tall.

"Enough out of you," Mrs. Cheever says. She tosses her plastic knife at Guy but it sticks between Abby's ribs. Guy stands elegantly on his bench, clears his throat and begins: "There's never enough happiness to go around to everyone at one time, so you older ones have to steal it from the young, and let the young die young, like you once did."

Abby is kneeling, catching her blood in cupped hands, saving it. She uses discarded paper cups, lining them up in rows to be filled.

"We could smoke in the bathrooms."

Mrs. Cheever jerks a thumb toward Guy and says from the side of her mouth: "Some people'll do anything for a spotlight."

"Okay, we'll make a list, what're the most important items of discussion?"

One woman leans forward, reaches past her husband to tap another man on the knee while her husband leans back, reaches behind his wife to pat a different woman on the shoulder. All around the circle, some lean forward, some lean back, tapping knees or shoulders, holding secret meetings. Someone taps Abby's shoulder, reaching past her mother's neck. It's Darrell White, charcoal creases added to his mild face, between his sedate brows. He looks at her. She fills another paper cup.

"The video tape is finished," the cameraman calls. "Come and watch the party on television!"

They turn their chairs, scraping the pavement, forming classroom rows. The hostess dishes up popcorn. The show is in color: a patio festooned with crepe paper and balloons, confetti in the air, a circus band playing, a circle of people sitting, chirping and laughing, they stand up together, the screen follows them to where they surround Guy, standing on a bench, tall and motionless. Two men grab his feet, two others have his arms. They tie Guy to a lounge chair in the middle of the meeting circle. The spotlight is on Darrell who says something, smiles into the camera, then says something more, unsmiling. No sound comes from his mouth. A silent movie. The band plays. Darrell's motions are jerky. He keeps looking around. He mouths Abby's name. The party guests stand around the lounge chair, spitting, breaking plastic forks, tensing their muscles, giggling, glaring. A close-up of Mrs. Cheever's age-spotted hands tying a cord around Guy's neck. "No more speeches outta this guy!" His face turns blue. The band finishes a tune. The guests stare at Guy. Then Mrs. Cheever yells, "Remember the man who makes it all possible for us!" A cheer, more confetti and streamers. "Speech! Speech!" The screen goes black.

They turn away from the television as the cameraman rewinds the tape. Darrell looks quickly around, holds his hand out to Abby. She rolls over and crawls away, leaving a trail of paper cups. His hand just grazes the back of her head before the party guests lift him to their shoulders. Mrs. Cheever leads the chant: "Dare-Rul, Dare-Rul, Dare-Rul ...."

From his vantage point, Darrell watches Abby cross the lawn, inch by inch. He balances carefully, holding onto the shoulders and heads below him. He says nothing. They stand him on the table, legs spread like a colossus.

"Wait there, Darrell," Mrs. Cheever says solemnly. "I'm gonna walk for you." She clutches the arms of her wheelchair. "Shhh. This is important."

Darrell shakes his head: No. He holds his palms up: *Stop*. Mrs. Cheever stands. "This's the easiest part. I've been standing to change the television channel for years."

She lets go of the arms of her chair, thrusts her hands forward, fingers pointed toward Darrell. His lips pucker and say *No*. Silently. His eyes moisten. She leans and falls toward him—her feet never move—and lands with her face pressed against the front of his pants. "Happy birthday to a wonderful man!"

Darrell opens his mouth, groans an audible sound, a horrible sound.

Abigail lies down in the bushes against the fence and twitches like a dying animal.

Soon the party broke up. Darrell stood by the patio gate shaking hands, smiling thanks. As Abigail wheeled her mother past him, he patted Mrs. Cheever's cheek and looked into Abby's terrible dark eyes.

Abby stared straight ahead. As she went by, she whispered, "Happy?"

Tears glistened on his face.

# -The Kind of Sadness Which Makes You Sad-

He says he'll bring me back to my car later. His small truck and my VW are side-by-side in the parking lot. This morning at 7 they were the only two cars here. Now they're surrounded. None of the other teachers have left school yet. The students sit under trees passing year-books around. It's warm and hazy and too quiet for an afternoon on the last day.

He drives, I lean back, eyes shut. The air from the open window dries tears from my eyes and cheeks.

He lives close to the school. In a small town everyone lives close. Except me. On my first day he'd laughed, "You're going to drive 40 miles from the city every day to finish your student-teaching *here*?" They assigned me to him—David Chase. I drove the 40 miles twice a day. One way I always felt better than the other. Why can't I just accept it—it didn't work. Not the job, the teaching was okay, but what difference does it make, I may never be a teacher, I may do it if I have to, I never think about it anymore, stopped thinking about it the first day, or the second, there were other things to think about. Yet when it finally came to ... what it *came* to ... it was just one of those fiascos. But the next time would have to be an improvement. He'll have to realize that and give it another chance. When I get an opportunity I'll tell him that.

Now at three sides of a kitchen table, Bonnie Chase and I watch the movement of David's fingers

with acute attention as he rolls the fragile white paper, lifts it to lick with the pointed tip of his tongue, then twists the ends.

I was already introduced to her. "Kerry—my wife Bonnie." Formal preliminaries.

They are at the two ends of the table, and I'm on one side. I can't see both of them at once. But I don't think either of them can see the other without also seeing me. He holds the smoke down wide-eyed, staring straight forward at her. She holds it in with eyes pressed shut. Then my turn.

"Suck hard," he says. "And hold it."

Immediately I need a drink of water.

"You took too much. Watch me."

His lips press on it, the way he looks when determined. Sometimes he's determined not to laugh at a joke he told, even after I get it and smile at him. He's been determined other times too. Determined *to*, and then determined *not* to. Or is *sad* a better word?

While Bonnie drags, I say, "Now that it's all over, you can tell me—I'm not a very good teacher, am I."

"I don't wanna talk about that stuff."

"I know .... I'm not cut out for this ...." I take the cigarette from Bonnie's limp fingers. "... teaching, I mean... of course, I meant teaching ...."

"Just a little ... good ... hold it, real low."

The smoke comes out of me when I say, "I never minded the 40 miles—it gave me time to think."

"It's always good to think. Use it or pass it."

It burns. Coughing doesn't help. The cigarette seems to circle the table and come back to me so quickly. I suck on it twice so maybe it won't come back so fast this time. "I'm usually a fast learner. I feel I should apologize. To someone. To you? But if we could—"

"You mean about what happened in class to-day?" he says, nearly too rapidly to understand, quick glance at drowsy Bonnie.

"No. *Oh*. Yes." We *were* in the classroom today ... but nothing happened. We were always in the classroom. That other day too. The big curtains were drawn as though there would be a film shown. The desktop was hard and slippery, cleared of books and pencils, and at first we were just sitting there, side by side on the teacher's desk. Sometimes I was the teacher in that room and sometimes he was, but it was always *his* desk. And he pointed out my nervous laugh, the same one he'd also been telling me that I used in front of the students. I'm not laughing anymore. Is it because I'm no longer nervous?

"You always watched me teach my classes," I say, "but when *you* taught, you didn't want me to look."

"See, not look. I wanted you to see, not watch."

"Watch what?"

"I don't know. I don't remember."

"Which watch," says Bonnie.

"You're forcing," David tells her. She stares at the tabletop without blinking.

"It's sad," I say.

"Yes, it's sad," he answers. "What's sad?"

"Sad stories are sad. You've told me lots of sad stories."

"I have? I don't remember any. I didn't tell stories just for their sadness."

"But it makes me sad when people are happy about something and then get let down." I take the little cigarette. I want to cough. I want him to help me cough: massage my shoulders and the back of my neck, pat my back and clear my head. I'd like to feel if his brown hair is as fine as it looks. I never got to touch his hair. Next time I will. Maybe soon.

"Did I ever tell about that?" he says.

"About what?"

"The kind of sadness which makes you sad."

"Huh?"

"What did I ever say to make you sad?"

"Oh that." My turn again—I've lost count—hold the smoke down, belch it out. "That was a funny day. I don't mean funny ...."

"Did I tell a story that day?"

"Not that day, but other days. And I could picture you perfectly when you told me about the time you were a little boy, all excited about playing the trumpet on television with a school choir, and then you saw the tape and they'd drowned you out, the choir did."

"I told that story?"

"It's funny I remember it 'cause I can't remember something else."

"What."

"Why I said it. Just now, I mean, why I remembered. Why I'm sad, I think. I can't remember why I'm sad. Just because it's my last day?"

"You tell me a sad story," he says. "It's only fair."

"Well .... I can't think."

"Here." He hands me the cigarette. It feels as if the smoke fills my back and shoulders like balloons.

"After all," I say, "a last day is different from a last chance. It *should* be. Isn't it? You know what I mean?"

"Use it or pass it."

I stare at the cigarette, then he reaches over and takes it from me.

"Yes, I have a story too," my voice says. "I was five I think. What difference. We were going to have a barbecue, my father and I, and he was happy. I liked it when he was happy 'cause usually he was nothing at all—I mean no particular mood. He'd look at me if I asked a dumb question. I mean look at me for his answer. But we were having a barbecue, and I was sitting at the picnic table outside, the barbecue hot beside me, and he came from the kitchen with a tray of hotdogs and mustard and ketchup and pickles and other crap probably, how should I remember, but he was proud of that tray. He smiled over it at me and was proud that we would have a barbecue together. Then he stepped on a little train I'd left on the patio and fell. The last thing I remember about this is the spattered trail of mustard across the pavement."

I touch his fingertips as I take the cigarette. He's soft there, the pads of his fingers, like a cat with no claws. "I used to have a cat I liked to sleep with."

"Is this another story?" he says.

"Could be. Not really. She got old and was squashed in the drive-way. She couldn't hear the car."

"I know a sad story," Bonnie says. "When you brought home that painting, the one in the living room. You liked it. I didn't. But I let you hang it there."

"Why did you think of that?" he asks. He looks at her. She looks back at him. Both of them are profiled to me.

"I want to take it down," she says.

"Go ahead." He closes his eyes to pull smoke from the shrinking damp cigarette. His neck is hard as he sucks.

I ask, "What's it a painting of?"

"A guy fishing."

"It's a picture of fog," she says.

"The guy *likes* to be in the fog."

"Like some people I know."

"Whatever you say."

"I betcha I could fix it," I say. "I took an art class once. I'd add a gull—no, two gulls. And a whale jumping out. And a hermit crab. No, two hermit crabs."

"A boy and a girl crab?" David says.

"Sure," I say sadly. "Why not?"

"Nothing can make it a better painting," Bonnie says.

"Okay," David says. "Whatever you say."

"Whatever," I agree.

"Just a minute," Bonnie says when he holds the cigarette out for her.

"Too fast?"

"It's pretty fast."

"Feel anything, Kerry?"

"Everything."

"It isn't *that* fast."

It circles, twice more, in silence, and Bonnie presses her forehead with her thumbs. David leans back, pushes back, unbuttons his shirt. I watch like touching: the skin on his chest, brown arms and light hair, a muscle which makes a smooth ridge along the side of his leg. Maybe I could reach around and touch the backs of his knees.

"Hey—when did you change into shorts?"

"Right when we got here."

Oh yeah, when he left me and Bonnie uncomfortably alone in the kitchen, nervously smiling, then she said "excuse me" and followed him into another room.

"I didn't remember."

"Sorry," he says. "What don't you remember?"

"Well, what're we talking about?"

"Something."

"That's for sure."

"I don't remember it either," he says.

"That's okay. I do. I feel like for a long time someone's been rubbing on me, on my spine in between my shoulder blades, rubbing with their knuckles, for a long time, and now I need ... what'm I saying, anyway? Have you been rubbing me with your knuckles?"

"Not for a long time."

We laugh. Bonnie doesn't. I think it's the funniest thing I ever heard.

"It's hard to remember. But David, do you remember ... anything? Anything about ... you know, *any*thing?"

"Probably," he says.

"The good parts? But there weren't any good parts. Were there? It was horrible. *I* was horrible, that's what you remember."

"That's not true."

Bonnie skips every other hit. There's a blur in between when I swing from him to her. Like I'm not turning my head fast enough.

"I'm sorry I called," I say.

"What?"

"I'm sorry I called ... you know, that night." I close my eyes. Urgent words are escaping before I can say them. This might be my last chance. Don't want to waste it. "You know, *that* night ... after that day, I only called to ask you *why* ... you know, that day, why it was so messed up— At first I wasn't sure what was going on, what you wanted, what I should do. But *you* were so ... I don't know, *driven* .... Was that what was so horrible? But then I made up my mind, it was *okay*, I *wanted* to, I really did, but you weren't so sure anymore .... That was the awful part too...."

Bonnie is face-forward down on the table, her forehead on her knuckles. Her hands are freckled. A tear drips out of her lashes to the table top.

"I just mean I'm sorry I called so *late* ...."

He offers me the joint on a pin, but I shake no, hand on throat. He looks at it, twirling the pin, both eyes focused there, says, "It wasn't your fault. One of those things."

"That can't be all you have to say about it!"

"You're young." He looks at Bonnie. "Just a sec." And he leaves, bolts out of his chair, thumps through the living room, a door slams.

She may've been stirred to life by the swift wake of his leaving—he split the thick air, blew her out of her chair. She stands, then becomes still again. *She's* still, the rest of the room isn't—the room doesn't stop turning even though my head stops moving. I stretch one arm straight in front of me on the table top and lay my head on it, watch her with one eye because the other is squeezed shut against my arm. She's one dimension. A cut-out paper doll against the yellow-flowered kitchen wallpaper. A picture I could put my hand palm-flat against and be touching everything at once: ceiling, wallpaper, shelf of cookbooks, clock with a chicken on it, and Bonnie Chase, as motionless as the rest, as touchable or unreal as any of it, no more so, no less, and she turns to ask, "Did he ever talk about me at school?"

"What." No question. My lips don't even move. I drool on my arm.

"I mean, did he tell you anything ... about *us*, about me, about ...."

"What're you talking about?" I raise my head, stretch my fingertips to the carefully rolled, untouched second joint he left on the table.

"What's going on, Kerry—*really*, I mean what's really going on?"

"Huh?"

She leans down toward me, face thrust forward, eyes gleaming. "Has he told you anything? I've lost him, haven't I? *Have* I?"

"Maybe you'll get another chance. That's what *I'm* hoping for. That's all we can hope for."

She cries prismatic tears, pulls me out of the chair without touching me. I rise as though I'm growing. She has strong fingers, when she does grab me—has me by the shoulders, the bones in her fingers grinding against the bones under my skin. She digs in. Also her eyes dig in, and she cries against me, against my breastbone, the hard part of my chest—but suddenly it's like paper there, wants to cave in, wants to let her cry directly against my heart. Her or anyone else, it doesn't matter.

I remember the first time I saw you.

### Band Director

In the spring I was an undergraduate working in the band office: sorting photographs, you know—alone, because it was hard to work photos when people were around. Too tedious to try to answer them. I was told to expect you—not inspect. But no name was offered: "A well-dressed guy, young-looking and clean-cut." They told me to tell you where to go.

"Hello?"

I looked up and saw you and thought, It must be him, the one expected: dressed well, yes, and clean. It's always a good word. It's what's clearest, sharpest, most vivid, distinct and perceivable—in a photograph.

"I'm looking for Mark."

"He's down in the practice rooms."

Oh, I can picture myself with that loose straight hair all around. I had long hair then. Maybe if you had asked, Why do you have long hair, I could've said, Because I'm a girl; because most girls have long hair and are successful with people—get the connection? Then I would've cut it.

But you didn't ask that. You said, "Where are the practice rooms?"

"I'll show you."
I cut it off in the summer anyway.


I didn't go out of the office. I pointed the way from the doorway. You smiled thanks. A clean smile, and I kicked myself for not having my camera loaded. I looked at the back of your head as the hall door swung open then shut, the slowest of shutter speeds—what I'd use for a full-moon shot to open the darkness, expose the details, illuminate hotspots. I remember the way you walked—not like a soldier, not even like walking. Like sliding on glass. And your hands: sturdy, clean! Again clean. They'd catch highlights in a photograph, even in a night shot. Then I thought: A new band director. And I knew if the university had consulted me before hiring, they'd not hire anyone else. Already I was planning and practicing the clicking of hundreds of photographs, a whole wall of them, to join the others in my room: A gallery, a hall-of-fame where each photo of someone was a souvenir to keep, where I could look them in the eye while they finally told me why I needed to know them, why I needed to know anyone.

All that was ten seconds, maybe a minute. But for five months I remembered you—a man with a smile like a window flung open. Even among recently washed windows, an open one is the cleanest. The easiest to photograph through also. And for five months I planned a portrait. I knew how to tone the lights to a moon-glow—how they would bounce back from the softest umbrellas, bathing you from two sides. No shadows anywhere. And my lens would cut the real-life haze, the dust that jostles in a light beam. So inside my camera there would be only you.

But it's always in September that everything starts. The hottest weather begins then. The grass on the football field where I marched with my trombone remained green only because someone watered it. Every day was brilliant-hot, everything seemed too sharp, colors too pungent. Every morning was a color photo taken with too many filters, turning a bleached-white sky into deep blue, giving buildings and trees bold contrast against it. Shade was black and sidewalks blinding.

When classes at the university started—and football practice, and band rehearsals—portrait photographs were due at the printers for programs. That was my job. But you had yours done by a professional, then you lost the print after he mailed it to you. I told you I should've done yours—there would've been extra copies. I did the drum-major's photos, and you complained: "There's black across her eye."

"No! Hey, if she looked into the sun she would've squinted."

"You were too far away from her. You didn't need the shot to be from her waist up." You were waving the photo around so much, you couldn't have really been looking at it.

"I had to get the whistle in the shot. I had to keep the uniform and her features *distinct*." I tried to take it away from you, but you held it too high for me, out of my reach, like a boy teasing a puppy. I said, "Hey, how

would you like to sit around talking about pictures of
*you*."

And then you smiled. I never saw you in the
*process* of smiling, and I never saw the sun *coming* up—
it's just suddenly there, muscling its way over mountains, around trees or through cracks in clouds. Your
smile was always somewhere waiting inside, on your
other side, like where the sun is at night.

"I'd hate it. Don't come at me with a camera. I
hate pictures of me. Look at Jo here in your picture of her.
She doesn't look this bad."

"Listen, it's never the photographer's fault if
someone looks dopey in a picture. Film doesn't lie."

You held the photo in front of your nose, but you
looked at me over the top of it. Then you tapped it
against my forehead. "Are you explaining or defending?"

"No, wait, I—"

You stopped me with one hand palm up: hold it,
whoa, halt.

"Are you explaining or defending?"

I looked: your hair colored perfectly for photog-
raphy under stadium lights, your brow, your eyes looking out from underneath, your cheekbones absorbing
the fluorescent lamp's hot highlights, the darkened
dents below each cheek, your chin without a beard, your
neck, streamlined arms and conductor's hands holding
a photograph I'd taken that wasn't awfully good now,
in comparison.

"Defending."

I sulked. We both knew it. I could've drowned in
it, but you were magic—a photo come to life. You
prodded my shoulder with your finger like a blunt nail.

And each time you touched me on the outside, something hit hard on the inside: ping! Like that.

"When someone has a bad day, I push more and more and more."

My glasses had slipped, so when I looked up, I looked over, and you were a soft focus. "Why?"

"To make you tough."

There were people in and out of the office, back and forth, between and beside. I didn't want to *be* tough if it meant I would have to give up the singing of my nerves when you strummed them. You had to leave and I couldn't preserve it: keep your smile thumping inside. The vibrations slowed. This was no action shot—the movement frozen in a blur to move forever. Transitory, intangible—unless I had a picture to look at. I sat in your chair with my camera between my legs. And I held tight with both hands, and I squeezed with my knees. Nothing but a light-tight box without you inside it.

You started something. I stared at my hands—yellowed from time spent bathing faces in photographic developer. If you had looked at the drum-major's photo and said "nice," I might've just gone home, cleaned my lens, mixed chemicals, picked an old negative, polished a face on glossy paper. Someone else. Anyone else. Not you. But you started something. You had to be my only model.

## Darkroom Chemicals

It was a place you never saw, but I took you there with me often. Down in my basement, a wooden workbench and a cement floor, film to soup, negs to print, people to meet.

I had kept my camera in my shako hat while I marched the halftime show. Then in the stands during the game, that perfect light, that perfect sky background were mine.

Through the yellow darkroom safelight, I chose a negative. You. Up on a ladder in the bleachers, you leaned forward toward the terraced band members. I cropped them out. So it was only you, a profile, saying something, pointing to your ear. I smiled in the yellow dark. You hated that picture when I showed you the proof sheet. "Destroy it," you said. But I answered, "No. It's a classic."

Blown up, burned into paper, and sunk beneath the calm, amber liquid, it was even better. In the background was the crowd, blurred splotches of blacks and whites. But the lights above were on your other side, so you were cut out, separated from that confusion with an outlined glow. It was also better there in the dark, under chemicals, than it had been on Saturday night. Of course, Saturday night there were five piccolos and three clarinets between my lens and you. I shot over their heads. If I'd called over the noise, you would've said "What?" or maybe "Go back to your seat." The chemicals made a difference. I was right there next to you, no clarinets, no piccolos, they were cropped out; no noise except the timer ticking. I jiggled the chemicals and your coat darkened, but your hair remained fair, and I could say anything to you without shouting.

The next negative was shot from the back—your back, the band's front—and you held your arms out straight on either side, bombarded by the last chord. I'd told you, when I gave you the proofs, "Look at this under the magnifying glass. Look at this timing."

You took it. I tried to picture the way you looked at it while I drained the developer off the print before slipping it in the stop-bath. You leaned back on the springs in your chair. I didn't have my camera; you'd said don't ever bring it into the office. Otherwise I'd remember more.

I had another negative loaded in the enlarger. This one from the front, directing the band. Yes, I was right, the hands were made for photographs. And the hair. This one I'd shot upwards, had positioned the stadium lights in a ring around your knees. The glow crept around your cheeks, shone in your hair, but your eyes were lost in blackness. Not the crinkles, though— I rubbed them in with my fingers in the developer, smoothing them outward like a sculptor does on a head of wet clay. The lines slowly darkened, and I could see the cheekbones rise, the dimples lengthen, the neck harden. But the smile was already there, had been there all along. I couldn't create it myself.

"You couldn't hate this one too," I said as the sky finally darkened into a warm-tone true-black.

"I hate them all," I heard you say.

I stared at you floating in the tray. There was nothing tickling inside me. You weren't the same down in the basement, in yellow solutions, as you were up in the light, in the office, on the practice field, or in the stadium at night. Maybe I didn't have the perfect shot yet, hadn't zoomed close enough. Others I worked on became and remained real in the chemicals, had smiled shyly when I said, "You know, you're so boring to know outside this darkroom, just telling me what to do, what not to do, what has to be done, what should be done, then 'Good job, good job.' I'm not a job." Then as I smoothed skin-tone into their cheeks and hands I asked, "Why do I waste my time with you?"

I moved you over to the clear fix solution to make you immune to hard light.

## Band Director II

The reason I was standing there talking, instead of in my position to start rehearsal, was bad enough. That guy, the skinny one with bony hands—you didn't know, you couldn't know—he had once told the virgin queen she didn't give him enough, didn't put out. I could tell that day on the field under the sun, under his laughing and jokes, I could tell what he still thought: Why did you leave me, I told you I'd change, I promised, I changed, can't you see, I've changed, I've changed.

I *wanted* to walk away, to roll in the damp grass and erase all traces, to say, "You see, people are so boring to know, talk talk talk, they never say anything new, always want something." What could anyone want from anyone else?

Then you, on your ladder, your podium, your pedestal, with the sun making points around your fair hair, called down, "Andy! Leave Toni alone. She's supposed to be on the field."

Leave her alone.

I cursed not because you were rescuing me, but because you didn't know. What if I'd gone up to the ladder and looked into the sun, blank-faced in direct lighting, and said, "He was my boyfriend and attacked me once in my parents' garage." Or what if I'd developed a picture of it for you: He had me backed up against his front, one bony arm a vise around my chest, pressing me flat. And the other hand raking against me like a claw, a crow's foot, a hook trying to pull my insides out.

Then, standing down on the grass with you on the ladder: would you stroke the numbness out of me again, make me thump for a second or two? And me without a camera. So instead I said "Shit," and I went out to my position on the field.

"It was funny," you said in the office afterwards. Lots of people there as usual. "You stared at me with your mouth wide. I had a hard time keeping my own face straight. Then you said 'Shit' with such stomach support that the band thought I said it over the loud speaker. You stalked out onto the field, wham wham wham wham. If you were a cartoon there would've been a baritone sax or tuba to emphasize each step. A final wham, trombone on the grass, arms folded, and eyes back to me, black and angry."

Then you touched my shoulder with your finger-tips. "Tell you what, when I have no one to pick on, I'll pick on you, okay?" Your fingers tightened, ground into my bones, breaking through my rigid muscles, and you laughed.

I remembered the laugh—felt it rub me inside but couldn't photograph it. Damn, I couldn't bring my camera into the office. I don't recall when it was, a week before, two days before. What difference? Three important frames were blurry, and I'd said, "I can't accept money for these prints."

"Let me see them."

"I'm embarrassed, they're blurry, fuzzy, I can't fix them."

"Let me *see* them." You snatched them out of my hands. I sat and looked at my yellow fingers. You sat in your chair, leaning back, unfairly graceful. Then you stood and leaned against a table near me. I watched with a corner of one eye. Without a camera, no need to keep you framed and focused. What could possibly happen? No one in the office looked at us, of course—nothing was happening.

You looked at the photos again. I did too, without my glasses, papers of fuzz, all grey. You touched my knee and said, "You can't be perfect all the time."

"I want to be."

"But no one can. No one is. It's impossible." A smile. I needed my camera.

"Some people are."

"No."

Once you told me you practiced everything you did to make it perfect. Except you never practiced knowing people. "You are."

"Oh ...!" Your laugh swept over me so it hurt and tingled and soothed and pricked—the same laugh two days or a week later after I said *shit*.

But it didn't last. And I knew it wouldn't.


**Night Photo**

I think I am out on the football field. I don't remember, after all, I'm asleep. You climb off the podium, down the ladder, out of the clouds. I am waiting with my camera.

"May I lodge a complaint?" I'm joking, of course, to bring an expression onto your face.

"You are a complaint." Your eyes do not crinkle, in fact are almost sullen.

I am impatient: "No, I'm tryna tell you—"

A pause: you take a hold of the back of my neck with one powerful conductor's hand, shake me like a kitten with a toy.

Now clearly against the black velvet backdrop you are outlined perfectly. Eyes set deep, looking, laughing from the inside out. The corners crinkle. A smile that stretches dimples into furrows and tightens neck tendons like anger might on others but doesn't on you, eyebrows arching up and out.

My mind begins to click thousands of photographs. I need flash-fill to see your eyes, lost inside unfocused shadows. I want to illuminate details.

"Stop it."

"Stop what?"

"The camera. I hate that camera."

"You don't understand this camera."

I can't stop. Endless film. I want every angle. Your embarrassment won't show in black-and-white.

"Forget I'm here. Forget me." Photographer's chant. I must've heard it somewhere. I don't remember.

"Don't. I hate the way I look."

"But I can make you look good. Hold still. You'll be blurry."

I move faster and faster, trying to keep my lens on you, trying to keep focus, keep exposure; and though you do not wiggle or dodge, together we whirl, parallel circles that never cross, one around the other. Good, a blurred background. Indicates action.

"What did you do!" There, over my shoulder, my house is on fire. It is unrecognizable. I reach for fresh film—color. The flames are pretty, red and yellow and blue and orange all mingled up inside. Dark sky, dark ground. I am fumbling in an empty camera bag. I left it inside, with the fire ...? Sun through my upturned lens sparked my film to flames.

"Forget it! Run!"

I don't hear you. Afterwards I remembered you yelled, after the sun came back up. But the fire is louder than you are. My camera is in there. I know you hate that camera. You never understood it.

I dodge flames and get past the door. You don't try to stop me. I thrash from side to side, tangled in my sheets, dousing the blaze. There's no smoke from this fire, but everything's as black as ever.

My camera is black, lens-up on a burning bed, fire in a ring, red, yellow, like sunlight, moonlight, stadium lights. I have to reach through to touch it, hot, blistering, but whole. I clutch it to me, pressing it to my chest, my stomach, a hot lump against my heart. Treasured photos inside. Photos I save but will never see.

**Band Director III**

We had an important rehearsal. I guess I knew that. But I was warm. Not uncomfortable ... *warm*, with just shorts, halter, trombone, sweat that made my skin shine. Why did I feel so set free? There were three boys, brown-muscled, bare-legged, hair streaked with sun. All of us felt it: sun, grass, skin, horns.

I melted. I stood front-and-center below where you directed, and gave in to the sun that made me rubber. They—those boys—pulled me, stretched me, flattened me then rolled me up and bounced me around like a ball. I forgot I owned a camera. I forgot you were up there. Two-hundred people were walking around on a football field, each hitting the ground at the same time with the same foot. We laughed at that, at ourselves, and they teased: "Trombone-Toni knows all the positions." I giggled, squirmed, could've rolled like a puppy on the grass, twisting an upturned belly to be tickled.

I guess we were screwing up the drills. Distantly I think I heard your voice giving instructions. Wasn't the loud speaker working?

One of the boys said, "This is full of shit."

Then I wanted to rush up to you and explain, he meant his squad, me, the others messing up. Too late.

"This is stupid," you said. "It's a *stupid* rehearsal. I'm disappointed in most of you. Some people have worked very hard for this, and they're making it. Some haven't done anything. Hey! What you just said about this show or this rehearsal, that's what I'm saying now. About *you*."

The three boys blinked and stared with owl-eyes. I squinted up there. The sun burned spots in you. I couldn't see, couldn't take a picture anyway, but couldn't see if your mouth was hard, your cheeks shallow, your eyes like black smudges.

You said, "Aw, you're not even listening. I wasted all that, didn't do any good."

I wilted. The three boys wound down then wound back up again. They rode me like merciless riders on a spiritless bronc. When you left, when you climbed down, you left alone. Fast. I couldn't see you through the mob of broken ranks.

What next? I wanted to follow. What to do? I *did* follow. Back to the office.

I keep following.

In the dark I am at the beach. My lenscap is on, and I carry my camera not by the body, but with my hand around the lens.

I am alone, and know it, but I hear you breathing. Just like back in the office when I slipped past you, but not unnoticed. Eyes on each other, we moved in circles.

The sand falls away under my feet, and my feet fall away under me, and I'm on my stomach on a dune. I cradle my lens, protecting it from the salt.

I wonder if I had smiled, would you have? I sat and never tried, and looked down at my yellow fingers. I heard you breathing. My eyes were drawn up like by a magnet. You watched my hands also, then slowly, so slowly, raised your eyes and slapped me hard with that look.

And in the dark I am at the ocean on the beach, my eyes pressed shut against the brackish sand. The yellow light, above and on my left, is not my yellow darkroom safelight. I know it for a second. It's the light on the porch of your beach house. But magic in the dark, it lets me see without destroying the photograph on soft white paper.

I hear you breathing.

Ivory figures on the ivory sand ripple in the amber light. The flesh smooth and full and solid—no claws or rakes scraping the other. Nor inside me. Instead the rhythm of the figures is melodic. And I hear you.

Everything was noisy and confusing after rehearsal. I tried to hear what you were thinking. No clue. No sign. No camera. I couldn't bring it into the office, remember? You barred me out.

But both of us had left the office in the afternoon. And my camera is warm against my chest, pressed there and protected. The waves whisper in the background, caressing our ears, and I still hear you breathing. I cup the lens in my hand on the lip of a sand dune, deftly remove the cap. Is it the yellow light flickering? The chemicals rippling in a tray? Or the muscles of the ivory figures. Contract and relax, back and forth, between and beside.

People were in and out of the office. I never noticed. I stood and backed away from you, ran into a chair, moved it, backed into someone who said, "Watch where you're going." I was not out of reach, and you hooked a finger in my pocket and jerked me forward; my head snapped back.

You said, "I want to tell you something."

Like magic to be watching through my lens and seeing the picture develop and feeling only warm and smooth where the hook-scar is. I hear two people breathing—breathing each other's breaths. A breeze off the water stings my ears. And something rings in my ears: you *had* tried to tell me something. You had your hands in front of your heart, palms in, fingers spread, like an orator before speaking. You shook them, made fists of them, shook again, then pounded the desk with one. You looked at me, and I, looking back through shaggy hair I hadn't combed since rehearsal in the sun and wind, watched and shook my head.

I watch through my lens. The sand makes a bed, round hollows for your shoulders and hips. I split the images and put them back together. I cock the advance lever. With one finger I toy with the shutter release.

"What," I said.

"Tell me what's wrong with me. What went wrong in rehearsal today?"

"Today?" I pretended I didn't remember. Maybe we were talking about it a week later. Or a month. Or somewhere else, outside the office. A stuffy bar? An unsteady boat? The light-flecked beach at night?

"Today was warm," I said.

The night is warm and thick to touch or taste, to hold in a photograph, to keep forever the throb inside.

"Not too hot."

"No, I mean warm. Good warm. Like warm-tone glossies. Comfortable."

Finally!     You hit the desk once more,     the two of you rise together into the air and bounce back on  the sand,     your lips tightened,     the ivory muscles flex,     lines deepened,  your neck hard-ened,     you shudder—together—over and under, between and beside. You are dancers with liquid joints yet quivering tight muscles. You're the looseness of helpless laughter, yet also the pounding of drums, per-cussive waves, a hugely pulsating heart sobbing for more room to expand. You explode toward each other and collapse to sleep limp in the sand.

And there it was—you smiled. "I hate pictures."

"I know. You hated the rehearsal today also."

"But why?" You took my arm and twisted it behind me, and twisted me around, your knees on the backs of my legs. I fell backwards against your hip—it pushed into a soft space on my side.

"No, wait, I'm tryna—no, I can't tell you. I don't know what happened."

You released me, and I collapsed, sagged, but did not sleep.

And the sand makes hollows for my toes and knees, and my heaving ribs. I push the shutter-release with my lens pressed against my stomach. It clicks against me—a thud with no ring.

And at home I souped photo after photo—of you, on the ladder, in the bleachers, even during rehearsals: your clearly focused eyes focused on something else, someone else, never quite vivid enough.

**Car Show**

You wanted to hear the tape of the band's latest halftime show on the finest sound system available. Mark, your assistant, had four speakers with his tape deck in his Volkswagen.

"When am I gonna not have to run my battery down while we hear these tapes?" he said.

"When you buy me a tape deck for my car," you answered.

"You've got money. That thing you drive that looks like a dump truck is a Porsche!"

"That's why I don't have any money."

"I don't even have a single-speaker radio," I said while stacking my books according to size. "Unless I count myself—I have to sing to myself while I drive."

"Plug the tapes into Toni," Mark said. "She'll sing them to you."

You clamped your hand like a vise on the top of my head, then pounded me like a nail with your other fist.

"Come on then, hurry," Mark said. "I've got things to do tonight."

"Like what?"

"Like things. Come on."

"Afterwards, you can buy me a beer."

"You already owe me a six-pack."

"Ho ho."

I went out of the office then, left you complaining or making bets for more beer, to get my camera from my locker and go home. That's why you were past the tennis courts and halfway to the parking lot beside the frat houses when I caught up, by accident. You were walking slowly, but Mark had stopped complaining, and Jo, the drum-major, was there.

We four were walking along behind the frat houses. You were like a colt, side-stepping, head tossing. I would have shot some photographs, but I had too many books to carry. I trudged along behind, watching. My camera bag slapped my hip to remind me it was there. Jo was giggling and bubbled over off the sidewalk.

"Watch it!" You pulled her back. But the car there in the alley had been going slowly. I thought it was parking behind one of the fraternities. It pulled up beside us, a shiny green fender, chrome hubcaps. I looked in, you kept walking. The eyes inside were bleak ... yes, that's the word.

"Hey, stay outta the road. I'd advise it." You didn't hear him, I don't think.

"Don't you know what life is?" I couldn't see that one—just that he had a beer can. I moved, the green car followed. Close, with those dirty eyes.

"Hey, you wanna stay alive?"

Three more steps. Only half a rotation for the white-ringed tires. You and Jo were shoulder-to-shoulder ahead, up past the headlights. Mark, by the back door, muttered, "Hey, what the hell, what—?"

The heavy-lidded eyes inside looked out at me. Beer in the back seat. I halted; likewise the car. I think you stopped and turned around, way up by the headlights.

"Hey, stay outta the damn road, I'd advise it. Stay ona side."

The green fender was dirty. The eyes said nothing, only looked. The words came from the back seat darkness. Gravel ground under black rubber as the green pressed closer. "You wanna know about life? Huh? You wanna live? Stay outta the road."

I was in the middle of a circle, the midpoint in a plane. You and Jo watched from beyond the headlights, way up there, how far away? Mark back behind the rear bumper. Way back there.

I see myself step forward, put an obnoxious hip against the green metal. I hear myself say, "Here's life for *you* guys"—extended middle finger—"you assholes, you fuckups, what do you know about living except swilling beer?"

They asked and I told them. What else were they following for? What is there to be so angry about! I hear the car door bang open, bouncing on its hinges. They are piling out, tangle of arms, legs, beer cans, eyes, fists. Whee, now we'll see! Now we're getting somewhere. I dodge and squirm and block their blows with my textbooks, slam my foot into bulging crotches. But I throw my camera bag to you and watch you run—and grin because there's magic inside, and this time *you* rescue it: an epic on film, black-and-white muscle and blood toned ivory without contrast. Trees fall, the earth shakes, the sky breaks stormy black. Shadows of people run, distant screams echo. Cars, lost in the density, collide and flame like far-away sparks, throwing dancing patches of dark and bright across the road. Down I go. I watch from the ground up. I smile victory as I join the dust. I know where my camera is.

Before I did it, before I said anything, you brushed past, crowding me away. I was on the sidewalk next to Jo. She said, "What's going on?"

Mark crossed the road behind the car. Two with faded jeans tumbled out on that side. I don't think he said anything to them. They had him covered from both angles.

You leaned in the window and talked to the sleepy-eyed one. Not a colt anymore, no switch tail. I wished I knew what you were saying. Slowly, so you wouldn't know, I set my books down and unzipped my camera bag. Then you shifted your position; allowed the sun to slide past your shoulder, trapping a drop of it on your profile, against the opaque blackness of the car's insides.

I watched through the lens, twenty frames untouched by light, waiting for this: The polished glass cut through the dust, the car, the bold light, the street, the

fraternities, the beer and the loudness. Just you remained, pale against a black night, and pale sand all
around, miles of it, and a yellow moon, two figures
wrapped up, between and beside, the glow of slow
motion, soft blurred action—and my heart racing inside. Prepared to take it all.

I lowered my camera and removed the lens cap.

When I next saw those sullen eyes inside, you'd
gone around to where Mark was flanked in the road,
where they told us not to be. You looked over the green
roof once, at Jo and me. She said, "What's going on?"

I was staring, eyes big as that sloping, tinted
windshield. Then I raised my camera again, narrowed
the field with a 250mm. Your lips moved, then a smile,
then moved again. Never both at once. They—the ones
in jeans—had clenched fists. The beer waited on the
green hood. I got it all in one line: green metal, beer can,
the two guys with thick necks and broad shoulders and
hard-knuckled fists, taking steps backwards, forward,
sideways as you talked. One pumped his fists up and
down at his sides, then shook them out into hands. The
other rocked, right leg, left leg, right leg. And you—that
smile, loose and relaxed, pale palms at your hips open
and turned forward: Hey, pardner, I ain't gonna draw. I
wanted to tell you to go ahead, *go ahead*, but I couldn't
get close enough. No lens was that strong.

Jo said, "What's going on? What're they doing?"

"I don't know. Nothing, I guess. Nothing, now."
Nothing would happen, it would never happen, it would
never include me. This shot was no good. I lowered my
camera.

You turned to leave, music in your pocket, looked
at us, an all-clear. Jo scampered across the road, daring

to step on it now, the turf you won. She bubbled again, relief.

My smile was small and aimed at my shoes. I didn't need to watch my hands as I wound the neck strap around my camera and tucked it into the red plushness of its case. The only picture I ever wanted, I didn't shoot. It wasn't mine to take. You might've even defied the film completely. Yet even if a photo could've held you, it would always just be you, and never me too.

I cut an angle across the road, through the parking lot, around the dusty cars to my own, the dirtiest. I looked back once, but couldn't see you. It was a wonderful show. Thank you. Not boring in the least, even though I missed the beginning and the end, and a few parts in the middle.

—————— Someone's Getting Mad ——————

He wasn't supposed to survive, born four pounds, so they named him Darwin. And he did live. When he was a rickety three-year-old, someone noted, measuring his wrists and ankles with thumb and forefinger, that it was a good thing modern medicine wasn't around during early evolution, because if people like Darwin had survived then, the human species might be extinct now.

"But evolution doesn't work that way anymore," his father announced (or lectured). "Look, Darwin can *read*." And over and over he shared the family's favorite story, framing and presenting it solemnly with swollen voice: Darwin was helping a neighbor with her laundry, handing her each clothespin as she needed it. She said, "You know, Darwin, my boys used to help me like this. So I put a letter on every clothespin, and as they handed each one to me, they told me which letter was on it. You could do that with your mother. It's a good way to learn the alphabet." Darwin's face didn't flicker. "My mother already *knows* the alphabet."


He said he didn't remember that story when it happened, and hardly remembered or maybe *didn't* remember when his father took his stuffed dog and bear away. He couldn't even remember their names, but he recalled sleeping with them, holding on, sometimes squeezing one between his legs. Then they were gone. He cried, or thought perhaps he probably did. His father might've told him afterwards, maybe years later, only sissies sleep with dolls; men don't. But he was positive about remembering his first baseball game.

They said to go out to right field.

"Where's that?" Darwin asked. His legs stuck out below the baseball pants, plucked clean like a chicken's legs below the plumage. His mother had pointed it out, and she worried about it.

"Just go out that way until I tell you to stop."

So he went, way out to where the grass ended. "Here?"

"Farther. Keep going. You're only on the baseline."

He walked more, until the grass started again, sparsely, like weeds. "Here?"

"Go on, farther, I'll tell you where."

Farther, he kept going. "Here?" He had to shout.

"I guess that'll do."

Right field was so far from anyone else in the game. The audience, his parents in the bleachers, were closer to the rest of the boys. But there was a fence nearby, behind him, where some goats stood chewing. He wanted to go to them, stick his fingers through the wire to be softly nibbled. But this was where right field was, and he'd better not move, not a step. Anyway, it was a goat's fault he couldn't have a pet—that's what he'd decided. He asked for a pet and his father said no—*he'd* had a pet goat while growing up and his folks made him take it to the slaughterhouse because they needed the meat. And the damn goat, his father said, *followed* him to the slaughterhouse. He didn't even need a leash.

Damn stupid goat. His father blamed the goat for getting killed, for allowing that to happen, so no pets. Darwin's mother bought him a fish tank.

A baseball rolled toward Darwin. He watched it. It couldn't possibly come right to him; it veered to his right, hitting rocks, hopping, bouncing; it wouldn't even come close. He watched it, kept his eye on it until another boy ran from somewhere, picked it up, threw it away, and ran back. The goats and Darwin watched. The goats missed a few chews.

After the game—after he had walked to right field several times, always finding the same spot to stand again, and then walked back when they called him—his father clamped a hand over Darwin's skeletal shoulder and steered him toward the coach.

"Maybe you could tell the boy what to do when the ball is hit to him," Darwin's father said.

"Ah, yeah, well ...." The coach thought hard. "Okay, throw it to the pitcher—*he'll* know what to do."

Darwin said nothing. His father talked to him on the way to the car. While his father drove, Darwin clutched the crotch of his baseball uniform.


He went to college, to the coast, where first of all someone mistook him for a prisoner of war who'd come back to school before losing the gauntness of captivity. Darwin didn't have cheeks, but below his eyes, if anyone looked closely, his cheekbones, tiny and fine, slept beneath his skin. His face was lean and straight and easy to shave, dominated by his mouth and large teeth. He also had no shoulders, or very little, and only his long

neck kept him from appearing to be continually shrug-
ging. And his arms were long too; anyone could still
wrap his wrists with thumb and forefinger; his hands
were made beautiful by slender, elongated fingers. And
if he was thin, so thin, too thin, he was all sinew. He
threw a baseball stronger, faster, trickier than anyone on
the coast, strike after strike he threw—then he ducked in
case they hit it back at him, but they seldom did.

They said he had offers, could've signed with any
team in the major leagues, could've practically written
his own contract (they said).

But he didn't.

And someone said he'd told them that a monk
had signed him up to sit on a hill, quietly.

He was probably partly joking, they decided.

He cabled his parents that he'd been killed and
his unidentifiable body had been cremated before they'd
found his papers.

He changed his name to Buddy.

Now he's holding his temper in the California
Sierras.

Forest maintenance engineer, ranger, game-
keeper, and many other titles describe his job. Wearing
an olive green workshirt and pants, boots and brim hat,
he has camping areas to patrol and several hundred
dense miles of surrounding wilderness. He softly spends
the day finding nothing to anger him, at night lies in a
forest service station, goes into town once a month,
surely no more, for ten years now, going on forever.

September, the end of the season, and the campers begin to thin out: first the big trailers in the lower sections, then the canvas tents up around 5,000 feet collapsed, folded, and headed home to Los Angeles or San Diego.

Buddy continued to be lean as most trees and preferred to pee behind one rather than use the outhouses. He spoke serenely, sang clearly, but never whistled because the thin air would bounce the sound from the face of every peak, bare and vulnerable above the timberline, disturb every bear, deer, and occasional mountain lion, driving them farther back into unreachable areas.

As always, two weeks before the first snows, he went to town to a girl in a hotel room who wouldn't touch him with her hands or suck him, but lay spread-eagled, head turned, ignoring his effort—work which was more rugged than what waited up the mountain: chasing and pulling the last brave wilderness dwellers from their two-week vacations, leading the lost out before the snow pack kept them there forever, and finding the body, at least one a year, dashed apart, broken and tangled in the brush at the foot of the silent palisade rock faces, which placidly watched him carry their victim away. The wind never stopped up there on the peaks.

The cold began early, the wind came down off the rock faces, driving the last mountaineers home, but Buddy stayed up beyond the roads, covering abandoned fire areas, kicking over rock piles, hiding evidence. One fire pit, ringed with rocks, was warm, and he pressed his gloved hands right down onto the dust of the embers. The owner of the matchbook, left on the biggest rock, had a red beard and small eyes behind glasses, a thick neck, and a completely prohibited shot-gun.

"We're closing the forest—no more camping until spring," Buddy said—still squatting by the fire, his delicate knees near his ears—as the grunting man stepped into the clearing. "And no guns up here—what're you hunting, anyway? It's not legal," Buddy said flatly while the man asked him to stand: tucked the gun barrel under Buddy's chin and lifted him. Still using the gun, not moving his hand from the stock nor the other hand from his pocket, the man spread Buddy's arms away from his body. He kept the gun pressed against Buddy's crotch as he emptied his green pockets, took his flash-light and canteen and snakebite kit, wallet and badge and his knife which hung from his belt. He never moved the gun. The man loosened Buddy's buckle, lowered the zipper, then used the gun to ease the pants down, and underwear next. Sweat in Buddy's crotch started to freeze and his butt blotched red and white and tightened to keep the wind out, but never shivered, and never twitched as the man moved behind him, slid the gun between his legs, the muzzle tight against his shrunken nuts, and lashed his flanks with a long branch, whistling through the bitter air and shattering against Buddy's brittle-cold ass, each mark first a bright red line, then death-white.

Whenever he made a fire, the snow softened around the fire ring; and in late spring the snow every-where softened, and the roads came up from beneath it. The winds up on the palisade shrieked over the snow packs. The creek coming down from the glaciers rumbled, roared bitter shouts of protest over being pushed too fast. So at first the motorcycle engine was protected, hidden by the nasty voice of the mountains waking up. Buddy stood in one sticky wheel-rut on the road, straddling the motorcycle's footprint. The wind came from everywhere, carrying the motorcycle's boast, an echo from every direction, a challenge. Buddy set up a road block and waited.

The boy on the bike never removed his headgear nor removed the goggles he wore inside it, but he slowed down, nearly stopped at the log in the road. As Buddy moved toward him, he spun, slipping in the mud, digging it up, throwing handfuls, mouthfuls across Buddy's shirt. The machine retreated up the road; Buddy followed, then tried to step aside when the bike came straight back toward him, but he couldn't step far enough, fell on his ass, spun there, crawled then slithered on all fours until his feet caught up and he ran upright, a large brown circle of frigid mud on his butt, slapping his flanks as he ran. The motorcycle hovered behind, matched his speed, clung to his heels. Buddy veered off the road into the sage and manzanita, leaping bushes which the motorcycle then plowed through, blowing bits of twigs out behind like exhaust. He turned again, cut back across the road, watched over his shoulder, running sideways. The motorcycle cut a wake in the loose mud. Buddy's breath grunted in his chest, wheezed like wind through his grimace. He broke through thicker brush, and the bike came after him like a saw wheel, the pitch of the motor rising as tips of branches wound up inside it. And finally it spun without power, stopped in its tracks, whirring hysterically, at the same time that

Buddy bashed through a final thick wall of limbs, tripped on a root, spun for balance—reaching behind with one hand—and landed (once again) on his ass. This time in the river. Where he stayed, his knees up under his chin, arms wrapped around them, the melted snow from the mountain peaks swirling around his waist. He watched the boy beside the bike pulling branches and leaves from it, long bare twigs and new grass. The helmet kept turning toward him, watching from inside, far inside, behind the goggles, a huge global head rotating on its thin axis. Buddy still refused to shiver. He felt himself withering, his nuts crowding to the inside. The boy turned the bike, gunned, and broke out of the thicket the same way he came in. Buddy stood and dripped.

There was a springtime sun, but incapable of drying anything. He took off his boots, stuffed his socks inside, tied the laces together and draped them over his shoulder. One boot kicked him in the ass. Took off his pants and underwear, put the underwear—stained wet brown in back—into a pocket, put the pants around his neck, one leg on either side, and tied the legs together to keep the slimy cuffs from slapping his groin. He tied his shirt tails together too, the knot right above the red tip of his penis which was pulling itself in and back like a turtle's head, hardly existing at all.

His hands were free. He covered himself with his hands like cups, made a loincloth, rubbed it from lifeless indifference to angry readiness. He held on, warming his hands, going home down the road beside the creek. Sometimes the mud came up to his ankles. He walked and worked at himself and waited—his breath fogging the air, sparkling there—waited to spill and see it steam in the mud.

His feet seemed too fat, too wide, splayed, felt nothing yet caught a rock deep in the mud which pitched him forward, landing knees first. He wouldn't let go of himself to break the fall with his hands—until it was too late to matter. He released himself, and his palms skidded up the road, embedding pebbles and sticks. He fell on his cock, and the road wasn't soft there. The cock bent, cracked a little on one side and some blood oozed down the shaft, but nothing bubbled— neither white nor red—from the top. The pressure inside it flooded back into him. He screamed and puked and rose to his knees—with one hand he held the rock which had brought him down. And he cried, mouth open with no sound, not for the pain in his dazed organ, but at all the wilderness looming above him, and screamed again from his long neck, guttural, his mouth wider than his face, hurled his voice from the sandy sage hillside to the timberline to the palisade rock tower, castrating the forest's perfection.

And he no longer held his temper—threw it like a baseball, like the rock in his hand which shattered a smooth place in the creek beside him.

He approached the river, feeding it each rock he passed, lifting and shoveling in a single underhand motion. Most rocks took two hands and the water exploded with their entry. Then every boulder, every boulder *every*where it seemed, he rolled, pushing with arms and hips, sometimes turning and pressing with his butt and legs, slid the granite through the mud, smash- ing bushes, and into the water. He ran up and down the bank—naked like a frog from his waist down, pants and boots and shirt clothing his torso—and collected every rock, every log, every loose branch, and a bird's nest from last year, took them into the water, wedged them between boulders. Then the bushes themselves, cut them off at the base—and clumps of grass with roots, mud still attached, replanted them in the river between the rocks. Or twirled them over his head like a sling, spitting mud, and let fly to splat against trees or skid into the water or mash onto the rock dam. He filled cracks in the granite wall with wood, smaller rocks, handfuls of leaves and finally mud, handfuls and handfuls thrown into the rocks, curveballs and fastballs, sliders, spitballs. Little loose drops of dirt hissed into the water and lumps of mud smacked like flesh against the damp boulders. He wiped his flaring nose with the back of his hand and enjoyed the fishy smell of fresh wintery sludge. He wiped his palms on his very white flanks.

The river spread out, up over the stumps of shrubs and the mud where no rocks remained, up into the meadow he'd made, spread flat and brown, bubbling sourly on the edges. He stood out of reach. As the wetness oozed toward him, he stepped back. The trapped water searched for the river bed. But below the dam, the creek continued, drained itself, abandoned the river bed, left wet flatlands sparkling in the cool sunlight, a prairie. Rainbows streaked across, and fishing line carried the sun like rays. And all this time Buddy watched, and watched himself swell again below the foul shirt and pants. His penis flexed itself under the dried blood and streaks of earth while he watched the creek suck at itself and watched himself grow, his rage evolved, the river destroyed itself.

Something moved, tried to slither across the pebbles on the dry side of the barrier. Buddy stepped carefully across the sandy creek bottom and began to toss the fish onto the opposite shore to see if they could do better. And they did. They flopped around. They stared up. They rested, staring. They gasped and whispered, moving their mouths without a word spoken. They waited, without blinking. Looked at the sky. Waited for someone to put them back into the water.

## Wistfully

Here's something I sort of thought about:

I was a virgin and he wanted to sleep with me. He was about fifteen years older than me, so if I was twenty, that would make him thirty-five. I wasn't his secretary or anything, nothing like that. We worked in a romance novel factory. He was an editor, I was on the assembly line. They usually gave me the second chapter—background and flashbacks. I got to read the first chapter but never got to see how the whole thing turned out in the end. When I'd been there about a year, quietly doing my job, we went on a business trip together. It was some sort of conference or convention in San Francisco. Over dinner the first night, he said he really hadn't been required to come on the trip, but came anyway to take care of me. He had an itinerary and I followed him around and he pointed out who's who and who to avoid and which ones were the leering old men hiding behind grey mustaches or bifocals. He pointed out women coming onto men, men coming onto men, men showing off for women. What was the convention *supposed* to be about anyway? What are conventions ever about. No one who goes will tell.

*How was the convention?*

*Oh, you know* ....

Of course some of the women he'd pointed out coming on to other men started coming on to him too. Afterwards he told me every word they said, my mouth hanging open at their unabashed gall. The more handsome the man is, the more audacious they become. I looked at him and noticed his wide-set direct bluish eyes, his flat cheeks and sturdy jaw and sandy brown hair, the quick smile, the lean neck, and he looked good in a suit, when he wore one, but lots of times wore tennis shorts or cut-off jeans, and had the legs to get away with it.

Then one night he disappeared and I found him having dinner with someone else. She was slightly older than me. Very glamorous. Her hair all piled on her head, sparkling ear rings, low-cut dress, apricot-colored silk or satin, thin gold bracelets on her arms, tasteful make-up with just the slightest hint of glitter in her eye-shadow. I saw them across the room but didn't go any closer. Skipped dinner. Went to my room and sat there. Turned on the television, but it was Sunday evening, early, nothing worth watching. I could've sat and looked in the mirror, but didn't. I knew what was there.

He knocked on my door around 9:30. I didn't say anything. It was open and he came in. At first we just looked at each other. I sat on the foot of the bed, he sat on the nightstand. I could look at him without welling tears, without blushing, without smiling, without guarding my eyes. But it was his turn to say something and my turn to just sit there. I never attempted to lead or beguile him. But before he even said anything, he moved over next to me and stroked my hair. He continued to touch me like I was some sort of beautiful animal. When I shut my eyes for a second, he said, "Sweetheart, I hope you don't have the wrong impression." Seems like a foolish thing to be called, until someone says it while stroking your hair, and you know you don't have to answer. He said, "Maybe I've been treating you like a little sister, but that's not what I want. I like the way you look at me and I hope I didn't do anything to change the way you see me. She's a friend of my wife."

I opened my eyes. Yes, I knew he was married. Maybe people don't really talk this way. I don't care.

He said, "This friend wanted to know why we're separated. It's hard to explain when you don't really know the reason in the first place. She was suffocating, she said. She has a career and no children, but was suffocating and moved me out."

"Is that why you're here?" I asked.

"Yes. No." He smiled, a little sadly. "I wouldn't do anything like this if I wasn't separated. But I'm not doing it just *because* I'm separated. Do you understand?"

I didn't have to answer.

"Don't be afraid," he said, "to tell me no or get lost or slow down or not now or you haven't even bought me dinner yet."

I smiled too, then said, "I'm only afraid because I'm ...."

"A virgin?"

"And don't know how...."

"To make love?"

"So it can't possibly be ...."

"Any good?"

"So you ...."

"Wouldn't come back—and you don't want it to be just another lousy one-night stand in the life of a newly separated asshole."

"Something like that."

"Exactly like that," he said. Already he knew me that well. "Whether we make love right now or not," he said, "I'll still want to tomorrow."

So he took me to bed. That's the way I like to say it. He had to sneak out at two or three in the morning and go back to his own room. There were people around who knew his wife. I guess she probably had worked in romance novels at one time. I lay there with the feeling you get when you know someone's thinking about you. Sort of like you know you'll never have to eat again. The next time we saw each other we wouldn't even need to smile. All our smiling at each other could happen invisibly, like touching someone's knee under a table. That's how I was sure it wasn't just a smile he was smiling at someone else that I mistook or had to pretend was for me. If this is corny, it doesn't matter. Sometimes someone says something is corny because it wasn't something that happened to them and they're ashamed to admit they kind of wish it had.

I had a great little house that I rented, in a quiet neighborhood with no all-night grocery on the corner, no one worked on cars in their yard or parked on their lawn. I couldn't give that up, of course, so I only lived with him part time. His apartment came furnished, the top floor of one of those new condo buildings downtown, near the park, a sunset balcony. The mosquitos and flies don't go up that high so you could sit outside at night. We had drinks on the balcony and I didn't hate the taste and he didn't get silly or sulky or anything, but he said wine made him gossip. He wasn't gossiping, just telling me what the other people at work thought about me. They were talking about me because I had quit so suddenly. I'd just stopped coming. It was real mysterious. But I had never *needed* to have a job. It had made everyone wonder, but along with the wondering, some of them finally said what they really thought of me. Of course they didn't know he would be coming home and telling me. They wouldn't've guessed in a million years that I'd be with him.

I started to cry. They'd blamed a lot of mistakes on me. He said, "But they're not thinking of *you* when they blame you, they're thinking of themselves—now *they* won't get blamed. Their purpose is to save themselves, not that they chose you to become a victim."

"But why *me*?"

"You weren't there."

"I know they all think I'm dumpy and kind of dumb."

"*Who* thinks that?"

"They do."

"You *think* they do. Do you think *I* do too?"

"I don't know, do you?"

It was just a temporary lapse. By the time he held my head in both hands and looked down at me, a long long look before kissing me, we were two people in a wine ad again. The sun went down and left us in some sort of flickery light, and a slightly damp, salty breeze crept in from the bay, making my skin feel and taste even more real. (He didn't have to say so.)

Sometimes instead of making love, he just held me. He would sing to me, or hum a tune. Everything

was going well for him at work, he was being promoted, but he didn't talk about work when he got
home anymore. The hours after he left in the morning
and before he came home in the evening went by in a
heartbeat, so it really felt like we had tons of pure
unadulterated leisure time to be together. Then I went
home Sunday mornings. Sometimes he called Sunday
night. I asked if he was doing his laundry or cleaning
the bathroom. It was funny because neither of us ever
had to do those things, but the bathroom was never
dirty and we never ran out of clean clothes. I didn't go
back until Monday afternoon, had my own key and let
myself in an hour or so before he came home. I always
left everything the way I found it and waited for him
out on the balcony—except the time his wife had left
a note on the refrigerator saying next Sunday she'd
bring the beer and he could buy the steaks. I took a
peach out of the refrigerator and a butcher knife from
the drawer and sat on the balcony shaving paper-thin
pieces of fruit and eating them off the blade of the
knife. The peach was gone when he got home.

When he came in the door, he called Hi and was
talking to me about something, asking if I wanted to go
out to the beach or a movie, went into the bedroom to
change his clothes, came out, still talking—not non-
stop like a giddy fool, just talking—but he stopped
dead when he went into the kitchen. I hadn't moved,
just heard his footstep from room to room, and heard
him take the note off the refrigerator then get a beer
out, but he didn't open it, and it still wasn't opened
when he came out to the balcony, but I didn't look at
him. He sat in the other chair and sighed. The peach pit
was on a little table between us. I had the knife balanc-
ing on the arm of my chair.

He cleared his throat but didn't say anything, and I brushed my hair out of my eyes but didn't say anything. He put his unopened beer on the arm of his chair and picked up the peach pit. I let my eyes follow his hand as he raised the pit to his mouth and when our eyes met, his hand fell. He rolled the pit around in his hand like it was a pair of dice. But we continued to look at each other. I wasn't shooting stingers and he wasn't dripping with apology and regret. The breeze was not as damp as usual, more like a warm breath. He glanced at the knife. He didn't bite his lip or shuffle his feet. I didn't look at him coyly or shyly or demurely or slyly. You couldn't hear either of us breathing. I certainly didn't sniffle or rub my nose. His eyes were beautiful, slate blue—not shiny or hard nor pleading—like distant mountains or the ocean on a calm day. Then he took a deep breath and blew it out slowly, closed his eyes for a second and tossed the peach pit over the side of the balcony. He looked at me and said, "By the time it gets to the bottom it'll be going as fast as a bullet."

"Then," I said, "imagine what would happen if I tossed the knife."

We both looked at the knife. There was a small piece of peach skin still on the blade. As I picked up the knife, he reached over and put a hand on my arm. I froze, the tip of the knife between my lips. His fingers tightened on my arm before he released me.

He picked up his beer and looked at it, then stood up and said, "I don't want this," and went into the kitchen to put it back. I got up too and went through the living room and out the front door.

I don't need to go into a lot of detail about the next two years. I backpacked around the country with a beautiful dog, an English setter, silver with blue flecks. My face got very thin so my cheek-bones became prominent and my eyes seemed sunken, my skin darker and slightly leathery. I wore tight jeans and moccasins that came up to my knees, a colored sarape, my hair got shaggy, dry, wind-blown. I spent as many nights in jail as I did on park benches or under a pup tent. I slept with truckers in exchange for food or a short ride. I went weeks on end without seeing any-one, composed fabulous songs while sitting in a spot of shade in the desert, then forgot everything—every word and every note—the next day, so I just had to start over and compose another. Went swimming naked with my dog. Got shot at by hunters. When I showed up at the office one day, barefoot, hungry, my dog full of ticks, I looked fifteen years older.

He was out to lunch. I waited outside and saw him coming, walking with his head down—not hang-ing, just watching where he put his feet, his eyes sort of blinking with each step. He looked like he had a tune stuck in his mind, lifted his head and saw me and stopped. By then he was only a few feet away from me. He had crow's feet at the corners of his eyes. The same color eyes. Almost the same color—just slightly faded. He didn't smile. Then he touched my face with one hand, like a blind man who sees with his fingers. Ran a thumb down my gaunt cheek, felt my darkened eye socket with the back of one knuckle, held my chin for a second in his palm, suddenly pushed all ten fingers into my matted hair and I shut my eyes the way a dog does when you touch it just right.

Anyway, that's just something I thought about last night before I tried to go to sleep.

# Is It Sexual Harassment Yet?

Even before the Imperial Penthouse switched from a staff of exclusively male waiters and food handlers to a crew of fifteen waitresses, Terence Lovell was the floor captain. Wearing a starched ruffled shirt and black tails, he embodied continental grace and elegance as he seated guests and, with a toreador's flourish, produced menus out of thin air. He took all orders but did not serve-- except in the case of a flaming meal or dessert, and this duty, for over ten years, was his alone. One of his trademarks was to never be seen striking the match—either the flaming platter was swiftly paraded from the kitchen or the dish would seemingly spontaneously ignite on its cart beside the table, a quiet explosion, then a four-foot column of flame, like a fountain with flood-lights of changing colors.

There'd been many reasons for small celebra-tions at the Lovell home during the past several years: Terence's wife, Maggie, was able to quit her job as a keypunch op-erator when she finished courses and was hired as a part-time legal secretary. His son was tested into the gifted program at school. His daughter learned to swim before she could walk. The newspa-per did a feature on the Imperial Penthouse with a half-page photo of Ter-ence holding a flaming shish-kebab.

Then one day on his way to work, dressed as usual in white tie and tails, Terence Lovell found him-self stopping off at a gun store. For that moment, as he approached the glass-topped counter, Terence said his biggest fear was that he might somehow, despite his professional elegant manners, appear to the rest of the world like a cowboy swaggering his way up to the bar to order a double. Terence purchased a small hand gun— the style that many cigarette lighters resemble— and tucked it into his red cummerbund.

It was six to eight months prior to Terence's purchase of the gun that the restaurant began to integrate waitresses into the personnel. Over the next year or so, the floor staff was supposed to eventually evolve into one made up of all women with the exception of the floor captain. It was still during the early weeks of the new staff, however, when Terence began finding gifts in his locker. First there was

I know they're going to ask about my previous sexual experiences. What counts as sexual? Holding hands? Wet kisses? A finger up my ass? Staring at a man's bulge? He wore incredibly tight pants. But before all this happened, I wasn't a virgin, and I wasn't a virgin in so many ways. I never had an abortion, I never had VD, never went into a toilet stall with a woman, never castrated a

a black lace and red satin garter. Terence pinned it to the bulletin board in case it had been put into the wrong locker, so the owner could claim it. But the flowers he found in his locker were more of a problem—they were taken from the vases on the tables. Each time that he found a single red rosebud threaded through the vents in his locker door, he found a table on the floor with an empty vase, so he always put the flower back where it belonged. Terence spread the word through the busboys that the waitresses could take the roses off the tables each night *after* the restaurant was closed, but not before. But on the whole, he thought—admittedly on retrospect—the atmosphere with the new waitresses seemed, for the first several weeks, amiable and unstressed.

Then one of the waitresses, Michelle Rae, re-guy at the moment of climax. But I know enough to know. As soon as you feel like *some*one, you're no one. Why am I doing this? *Why*?

So, you'll ask about my sexual history but won't think to inquire about the previous encounters I *almost* had, or *never* had: it wasn't the old ships-in-the-night tragedy, but let's say I had a ship, three or four years ago, the ship of love, okay? So once when I had a lot of wind in my sails (is this a previous sexual experience yet?), the captain sank the vessel when he started saying stuff like, "You're not ever going to be the most important thing in someone else's life unless it's something like he kills you—and then only if he hasn't killed anyone else yet nor knocked people off for a living—otherwise no one's the biggest deal in anyone's life but their

ported to management that Terence had made inappropriate comments to her during her shift at work. Terence said he didn't know which of the waitresses had made the complaint, but also couldn't remember if management had withheld the name of the accuser, or if, when told the name at this point, he just didn't know which waitress she was. He said naturally there was a shift in decorum behind the door to the kitchen, but he wasn't aware that anything he said or did could have possibly been so misunderstood. He explained that his admonishments were never more than half-serious, to the waitresses as well as the waiters or busboys: "Move your butt," or "One more mix-up and you'll be looking at the happy end of a skewer." While he felt a food server should appear unruffled, even lan-

own." Think about that. He may've been running my ship, but it turns out he was navigating by remote control. When the whole thing blew up, *he* was unscathed. Well, now I try to live as though I wrote that rule, as though it's *mine*. But that hasn't made me like it any better.

There are so many ways to humiliate someone. Make someone so low they leave a snail-trail. Someone makes a joke, you don't laugh. Someone tells a story—a personal story, something that mattered—you don't listen, you aren't moved. Someone wears a dance leotard to work, you don't notice. But underneath it all, you're planning the real humiliation. The symbolic humiliation. The humiliation of humiliations. Like I told you, I learned this before, I already know the *type*: he'll be remote, cool,

guid, on the floor, he pointed out that movement was brisk in the kitchen area, communication had to get the point across quickly, leaving no room for confusion or discussion. And while talking and joking on a personal level was not uncommon, Terence believed the waitresses had not been working there long enough for any conversations other than work-related, but these included light-hearted observations: a customer's disgusting eating habits, vacated tables that appeared more like battlegrounds than the remains of a fine dinner, untouched expensive meals, guessing games as to which couples were first dates and which were growing tired of each other, whose business was legitimate and whose probably dirty, who were wives and which were the mistresses, and, of course, the rude distant—*seeming* to be gentle and tolerant but actually cruelly indifferent. It'll be great fun for him to be aloof or preoccupied when someone is in love with him, genuflecting, practically prostrating herself. If he doesn't respond, she can't say he hurt her, she never got close enough. He'll go on a weekend ski trip with his friends. She'll do calisthenics, wash her hair, shave her legs, and wait for Monday. Well, not *this* time, no sir. Terence Lovell is messing with a sadder-but-wiser chick.

customers. Everyone always had rude-customer stories to trade. Terence had devised a weekly contest where each food server produced their best rude-customer story on a 3x5 card and submitted it each Friday. Terence then judged them and awarded the winner a specially made shish-kebab prepared after the restaurant had closed, with all of the other waiters and waitresses providing parodied royal table service, even to the point of spreading the napkin across the winner's lap and dabbing the corners of his or her mouth after each bite.

The rude-customer contest was suspended after the complaint to management. However, the gifts in his locker multiplied during this time. He continued to tack the gifts to the bulletin board, whenever possible: the key chain with a tiny woman's high-heeled shoe, the 4x6 plaque with a poem printed over a misty photograph of a dense green moss-covered forest, the single black fish-net stocking. When he found a pair of women's underwear in his locker, instead of tacking them to the bulletin board, he hung them on the inside door-knob of the woman's restroom. That was the last gift he found in his locker for a while. Within a week he received in the mail the same pair of women's underwear.

Since the beginning of the new staff, the restaurant manager had been talking about having a staff party to help the new employees feel welcome and at ease with the previous staff. But in the confusion of settling in, a date had never been set. Four or five months after the waitresses began work,

Yes, I was one of the first five women to come in as food servers, and I expected the usual resistance—the dirty glasses and ash-strewn linen on our tables (before the customer was seated), planting long hairs in the salads, cold soup, busboys delivering tips that appeared to have been left

the party had a new purpose: to ease the tension caused by the complaint against Terence. So far, nothing official had been done or said about Ms. Rae's allegations.

During the week before the party, which was to be held in an uptown nightclub with live music on a night the Imperial Penthouse was closed, Terence asked around to find out if Michelle Rae would be attending. All he discovered about her, however, was that she didn't seem to have any close friends on the floor staff.

Michelle did come to the party. She wore a green strapless dress which, Terence remembered, was unbecomingly tight and, as he put it, made her rump appear too ample. Her hair was in a style Terence described as finger-in-a-light-socket. Terence believed he probably would not have noticed

on greasy plates or in puddles of gravy on the tablecloth. I could stand those things. It was like them saying, "We know you're here!" But no, not *him*. *He* didn't want to return to the days of his all-male staff. Why would he want that? Eventually he was going to be in charge of an all-woman floor. Sound familiar? A harem? A pimp's stable? He thought it was so hilarious, he started saying it every night: "Line up, girls, and pay the pimp." Time to split tips. See what I mean? But he only flirted a little with them to cover up the obviousness of what he was doing to me. Just a few weeks after I started, I put a card on the bulletin board announcing that I'm a qualified aerobic dance instructor and if anyone was interested, I would lead an exercise group before work. My card wasn't there three hours before

Michelle at all that night if he were not aware of the complaint she had made. He recalled that her lipstick was the same shade of red as her hair and there were red tints in her eye shadow.

Terence planned to make it an early evening. He'd brought his wife, and, since this was the first formal staff party held by the Imperial Penthouse, had to spend most of the evening's conversation in introducing Maggie to his fellow employees. Like any ordinary party, however, he was unable to remember afterwards exactly what he did, who he talked to, or what they spoke about, but he knew that he did not introduce his wife to Michelle Rae.

Terence didn't see Maggie go into the restroom. It was down the hall, toward the kitchen. And he didn't see Michelle Rae follow her. In

someone (and I don't need a detective) had crossed out "aerobic" and wrote "erotic," and he added a price per session! I had no intention of charging anything for it since I go through my routine everyday anyway, and the more the merrier is an aerobic dance motto—we like to share the pain. My phone number was clear as day on that card—if he was at all intrigued, he could've called and found out what I was offering. I've spent ten years exercising my brains out. Gyms, spas, classes, health clubs ... no bars. He could've just once picked up the phone, I was always available, willing to talk this out, come to a settlement. He never even tried. Why should he? He was already king of Nob Hill. You know that lowlife bar he goes to? If anyone says how he was such an amiable and genial supervisor ... you bet

fact, no one did. Maggie returned to the dance area with her face flushed, breathing heavily, her eyes filled with tears, tugged at his arm and, with her voice shaking, begged Terence to take her home. It wasn't until they arrived home that Maggie told Terence how Michelle Rae had come into the restroom and threatened her. Michelle had warned Mrs. Lovell to stay away from Terence and informed her that she had a gun in her purse to help *keep* her away from Terence.

Terence repeated his wife's story to the restaurant manager. The manager thanked him. But, a week later, after Terence had heard of no further developments, he asked the manager what was going to be done about it. The manager said he'd spoken with both Ms. Rae and Mrs. Lovell, separately, but Ms. Rae denied the incident, and, as Mrs.

he was genial, he was halfway drunk. It's crap about him being a big family man. Unless his living room had a pool table, those beer mirrors on the wall, and the sticky brown bar itself—the wood doesn't even show through anymore, it's grime from people's hands, the kind of people who go there, the same way a car's steering wheel builds up that thick hard black layer which gets sticky when it rains and you can cut it with a knife. No, his house may not be like that, but he never spent a lot of time at his house. I know what I'm talking about. He'll say he doesn't remember, but I wasn't ten feet away while he was flashing his healthy salary (imported beer), and he looked right through me—no, *not* like I wasn't there. When a man looks at you the way he did at me, he's either ignoring you or undress-

Lovell did not actually see any gun, he couldn't fire an employee simply on the basis of what another employee's wife said about her, especially with the complaint already on file, how would that look? Terence asked, "But isn't there some law against this?" The manager gave Terence a few days off to cool down.

ing you with his eyes, but probably *both*. And that's just what he did and didn't stop there. He's not going to get away with it.

The Imperial Penthouse was closed on Mondays, and most Monday evenings Terence went out with a group of friends to a local sports bar. Maggie Lovell taught piano lessons at home in the evenings, so it was their mutual agreement that Terence go out to a movie or, more often, to see a football game on television. On one such evening, Maggie received a phone call from a woman who said she was calling from

Wasn't it his idea to hire us in the first place? No, he wasn't there at the interview, but looked right at me my first day, just at me while he said, "You girls probably all want to be models or actresses. You don't give *this* profession enough respect. Well," he said, "you will." Didn't look at anyone else. He meant me. I didn't fail to notice, either, I was the only one with red hair. Not dull auburn ... flaming red. They always as-the restaurant—there'd been a small fire in one of the storage rooms and the manager was requesting that Terence come to the restaurant and help survey the damage. Mrs. Lovell told the caller where Terence was.

The Imperial Penthouse never experienced any sort of fire, and Terence could only guess afterwards whether or not that was the same Monday evening that Michelle Rae came to the sports bar. At first he had considered speaking to her, to try to straighten out what was becoming an out-of-proportion misunderstanding. But he'd already been there for several hours-- the game was almost over- -and he'd had three or four beers. Because he was, therefore, not absolutely certain what the outcome would be if he talked to her, he checked his impulse to confront Ms. Rae, and,

sume, don't they? You know, the employee restrooms were one toilet each for men and women, all the customary holes drilled in the walls, stuffed with paper, but if one restroom was occupied, we could use the other, so the graffiti was heterosexual, a dialogue. It could've been healthy, but he never missed an opportunity. I'd just added my thoughts to an on-going discussion of the growing trend toward androgyny in male rock singers—they haven't yet added breasts and aren't quite at the point of cutting off their dicks—and an hour later, there it was, the thick black ink pen, the block letters: "Let's get one thing clear—do you women want it or *not*? Just what is the *thrust* of this conversation?" What do you *call* an attitude like that? And he gets *paid* for it! You know,

in fact, did not acknowledge her presence.

When a second complaint was made, again charging Terence with inappropriate behavior and, this time, humiliation, Terence offered to produce character witnesses, but before anything came of it, a rape charge was filed with the district attorney and Terence was brought in for questioning. The restaurant suspended Terence without pay for two weeks. All the waitresses, except Ms. Rae, were interviewed, as well as several ex-waitresses—by this time the restaurant was already experiencing some turnover of the new staff. Many of those interviewed reported that Michelle Rae had been asking them if they'd slept with Terence. In one case Ms. Rae was said to have told one of her colleagues that she, Michelle, knew all about her co-worker's

after you split a tip with a busboy, bartender, and floor captain, there's not much left. *He* had an easy answer: earn bigger tips. *Earn* it, work your *ass* off for it, you know. But who's going to tip more than 15% unless .... Well, unless the waitress wears no underwear. He even said that the best thing about taking part of our tip money was it made us move our asses that much prettier. There was another thing he liked about how I had to earn bigger tips—reaching or bending. And then my skirt was "mysteriously," "accidentally" lifted from behind, baring my butt in front of the whole kitchen staff. He pretended he hadn't noticed. Then winked and smiled at me later when I gave him his share of my tips. Told me to keep up the good work. Used the word *ass* every chance he got in my presence for weeks after-affair with the floor captain. Some of the waitresses said that they'd received phone calls on Mondays; an unidentified female demanded to know if Terence Lovell was, at that moment, visiting them. A few of those waitresses assumed it was Michelle Rae while others said they'd thought the caller had been Mrs. Lovell.

wards. Isn't this sexual harassment yet?

When the district attorney dropped the rape charge for lack of evidence, Michelle Rae filed suit claiming harassment, naming the restaurant owner, manager and floor captain. Meanwhile Terence began getting a series of phone calls where the caller immediately hung up. Some days the phone seemed to ring incessantly. So once, in a rage of frustration, Terence grabbed the receiver and made a

Of course I was scared. He knew my work schedule, and don't think he didn't know where I live. Knew my days off, when I'd be asleep, when I do my aerobic dance routine every day. I don't mind *who*ever wants to do aerobic dance with me—but it has to be at my place where I've got the proper flooring and music. It was just an idle, general invitation—an announce-

list of threats—the worst being, as he remembered it, "kicking her lying ass clear out of the state"— before realizing the caller hadn't hung up that time. Believing the caller might be legitimate—a friend or a business call—Terence quickly apologized and began to explain, but the caller, who never gave her name, said, "Then I guess you're not ready." When Terence asked her to clarify—ready for what?—she said, "To meet somewhere and work this out. To make my lawsuit obsolete garbage. To do what you really want to do to me. To finish all this."

Terence began refusing to answer the phone himself, relying on Maggie to screen calls, then purchasing an answering machine. As the caller left a message, Terence could hear who it was over a speaker, then he could decide whether or not to pick up the phone and

ment—I wasn't *begging* ... *any*one, him included, could come once or keep coming, that's all I meant, just harmless, healthy exercise. Does it mean I was looking to start my dancing career in that palace of high-class entertainment *he* frequents? Two pool tables, a juke box and big-screen TV. What a lousy front—looks exactly like what it really *is*, his lair, puts on his favorite funky music, his undulating blue and green lights, snorts his coke, dazzles his partner—his doped-up victim—with his moves and gyrations, dances her into a corner and rapes her before the song's over, up against the wall—*that* song's in the juke box too. You think I don't *know*? I was having a hassle with a customer who ordered rare, complained it was overdone, wanted it *rare*, the cook was busy, so Terence grabs another steak and throws it on the

speak to the party directly. He couldn't disconnect the phone completely because he had to stay in touch with his lawyer. The Imperial Penthouse was claiming Terence was not covered on their lawsuit insurance because he was on suspension at the time the suit was filed.

When he returned to work there was one more gift in Terence's locker: what looked like a small stiletto switchblade, but, when clicked open, turned out to be a comb. A note was attached, unsigned, which said, "I'd advise you to get a gun."

Terence purchased the miniature single-cartridge hand gun the following day. After keeping it at work in his locker for a week, he kept it, unloaded, in a dresser drawer at home, unable to carry it to work every day, he said, because the outline of the gun was clearly recognizable in the pocket of his tux pants.

grill—tsss on one side, flips it, tsss on the other—slams it on a plate. "Here, young lady, you just dance this raw meat right out to that john." I said I don't know how to dance. "My dear," he said, "*ev-ery*one knows how to dance, it's all a matter of moving your ass." Of course the gun was necessary! I tried to be reasonable. I tried everything!

One Monday evening as Terence was leaving the sports bar—not drunk, but admittedly not with his sharpest wits either—three men stopped him. Terence was in a group with another man and three women, but, according to the others, the culprits ignored them, singling out Terence immediately. It was difficult for Terence to recall what happened that night. He believed the men might've asked him for his wallet, but two of the others with him say the men didn't ask for anything but were just belligerent drunks looking for a fight. Only one member of Terence's party remembered anything specific that was said, addressed to Terence: "Think you're special?" If the men had been attempting a robbery, Terence decided to refuse, he said, partly because he wasn't fully sober, and partly because it appeared the at-

Most people—you just don't know what goes on back there. You see this stylish, practically regal man in white tie and tails, like an old fashioned prince ... or Vegas magician ... but back there in the hot, steamy kitchen, what's *wrong* with him? Drunk? Drugs? He played sword fight with one of the undercooks, using the longest skewers, kept trying to jab each other in the crotch. The chef yelled at the undercook, but Terence didn't say a word, went to the freezer, got the meatballs out, thawed them halfway in the microwave, then started threading them onto the skewer. Said it was an ancient custom, like the Indians did with scalps, to keep trophies from your victims on your weapon. He added vegetables in between the meatballs—whole bell peppers, whole onions, even whole eggplant,

tackers had no weapons. In the ensuing fight—which, Terence said, happened as he was running down the street, but was unsure whether he was chasing or being chased—Terence was kicked several times in the groin area and sustained several broken ribs. He was hospitalized for two days.

Maggie Lovell visited Terence in the hospital once, informing him that she was asking her parents to stay with the kids until he was discharged because she was moving into a motel. She wouldn't tell Terence the name of the motel, insisting she didn't want anyone to know where she was, not even her parents, and besides, she informed him, there probably wouldn't even be a phone in her room. Terence, drowsy from pain killers, couldn't remember much about his wife's visit. He had vague recollections of her leav-

started dousing the whole thing with brandy. His private bottle? Maybe. He said we should put it on the menu, he wanted someone to order it, his delux kebab. He would turn off all the chandeliers and light the dining room with the burning food. Then he stopped. He and I were alone! He said, "The only thing my delux kebab needs is a fresh, ripe tomato." Isn't this incredible! He wanted to know how I would like to be the next juicy morsel to be poked onto the end of that thing. He was still pouring brandy all over it. Must've been a gallon bottle, still half full when he put it on the counter, twirled the huge shish-kebab again, struck his sword fighting pose and cut the bottle right in half. I can hardly believe it either. When the bottle cracked open, the force of the blow made the brandy shoot out, like the bottle

ing through the window, or leaning out the window to pick flowers, or slamming the window shut, but when he woke the next day and checked, he saw that the window could not be opened. Terence never saw his wife again. Later he discovered that on the night of his accident there had been an incident at home. Although Terence had instructed his eight-year-old son not to answer the phone, the boy had forgotten, and, while his mother was giving a piano lesson, he picked up the receiver just after the machine had clicked on. The entire conversation was therefore recorded. The caller, a female, asked the boy who he was, so he replied that he was Andy Lovell. "The heir apparent," the voice said softly, to which Andy responded, "What? I mean, pardon?" There was a brief pause, then the caller said, "I'd really like to get rid of your

had opened up and spit— it splattered the front of my skirt. In the next second his kebab was in flames—maybe he'd passed it over a burner, I don't know, he was probably *breathing* flames by then—so naturally as soon as he pointed the thing at me again, my skirt ignited, scorched the hair off my legs before I managed to drop it around my feet and kick it away. What *wouldn't* he do? Looks like he'd finally gotten me undressed. It's ironic, isn't it, when you see that news article about him—I taped it to my mirror—and how about that headline, "Pomp and Circumstance Part of the Meal." There sure were some circumstances to consider, all right. Like he could rape me at gunpoint any time he wanted, using that cigarette lighter which looks like a fancy pistol. I wanted something to always remind me what to

mom so your dad could fuck me. If you're halfway like him, maybe I'll let you fuck me too." There is another pause on the tape. Investigators disagree as to whether it is the caller's breathing or the boy's that can be heard. The boy's voice, obviously trembling, then said, "What?" The female caller snapped, "Tell your dad someone's going to be killed."

watch out for, but I didn't take the lighter. Why not? I'll kick myself forever for that. There was so much to choose from. Now one of his red satin cummerbunds hangs over my bed while he still has the lighter and can still use it!

During Terence's convalescence, the Imperial Penthouse changed its format and operated without a floor captain, using the standard practice of a hostess who seated the guests and waitresses assigned to tables to take orders and serve meals. The restaurant's menu was also changed and now no longer offered flaming meals. When Terence returned to work he was given a position as a regu-

When he said "staff meeting," he didn't mean what he was supposed to mean by it. You know, there was a cartoon on the bulletin board, *staff meeting*, two sticks shaking hands, very funny, right? But long ago someone had changed the drawing, made the two sticks flaming shish-kebabs on skewers. So the announcement of the big meeting was a xerox of that cartoon, but enlarged, tacked to the

lar waiter, even though by this time most of the male food servers had left the restaurant and were replaced with women. Michelle Rae was given a lunch schedule, ten to three, Wednesday through Sunday. Terence would call the restaurant to make sure she'd clocked out before he arrived for the dinner shift.

During the first week he was back at work, Terence came home and found that his wife had returned to get the children. In a few days she sent a truck for the furniture, and the next communication he had with her was the divorce suit—on grounds of cruel and unusual adultery.

women's restroom door. *Be There Or Be Square! Yes, You'll Be Paid For Attending!* You bet! It was held at that tavern. Everyone may've been invited, but I'm the one he wanted there. There's no doubt in my mind. What good was I to him merely as an employee? I had to see the real Terence Lovell, had to join the inner-most core of his life. Know what? It was a biker hang-out, that bar, a biker gang's headquarters. One or two of them were always there with their leather jackets, chains, black grease under their fingernails (or dried blood), knives eight inches long. They took so many drugs you could get high just lying on the reeking urine-soaked mattress in the back. That's where the initiations were. No one just *lets* you in. Know what he said the first day we started working, the first day of the women food servers, he said, "You don't just work here to earn a salary, you have to *earn* the right to work here!" So maybe I was naive to trust him. To ever set one foot in that bar without a suspicion of what could happen to me. That same ordinary old beer party going on in front—same music, same dancing, same clack of pool balls and whooping laughter—you'd never believe the scene in the back room. It may've looked like a typical orgy at first—sweating bodies moving in rhythm, groaning, changing to new contorted positions, shouts of encouragement, music blaring in the background. But wait, nothing ordinary or healthy like that for the girl who was chosen to be the center of his dark side—she'll have to be both the cause and cure for his violent ache, that's why he's been so relentless, so obsessed, so insane ... he was driven to it, to the point where he had to paint the tip of his hard-on with 150 proof whiskey then use the fancy revolver to ignite it, screaming—not like any sound he ever made before—until he extinguished it in the girl of his unrequited dreams. *Tssss.*

The only thing left in Terence's living room was the telephone and answering machine. When the phone rang one Monday afternoon, Terence answered and, as instructed by his attorney, turned on the tape recorder:

caller: It's me, baby.
Lovell: Okay . . . .
caller: You've been ignoring me lately.
Lovell: What do you want now?
caller: Come on, now, Terry!
Lovell: Look, let's level with each other.

How can we end
this? What do I
have to do?

caller: If it's going to end,
the ending has to
be *better* than if it
continued.

Lovell: Pardon?

caller: A bigger deal. A
big bang. You
ever heard of the
big bang theory?

Lovell: The beginning of
the universe?

caller: Yeah, but the big
bang, if it started
the whole uni-
verse, it also *ended*
something. It
may've started
the universe, but
what did it end?
What did it *oblit-
erate*?

Lovell: I still don't know
what you want.

caller: What do *you*
want, Terry?

Lovell: I just want my life
to get back to nor-
mal.

caller: Too late. I've
changed your life,

haven't I? Good.

Lovell: Let's get to the point.

caller: You sound anxious. I love it. You ready?

Lovell: Ready for what?

caller: To see me. To end it. That's what you wanted, wasn't it? Let's create the rest of your life out of our final meeting.

Lovell: If I agree to meet, it's to talk, not get married.

caller: Once is all it takes, baby. *Bang.* The rest of your life will start. But guess who'll still be there at the center of everything you do. Weren't you going to hang out at the bar tonight?

Lovell: Is that where you want to meet?

caller: Yeah, your turf.

Terence estimated he sat in his empty living room another hour or so, as twilight darkened the windows, holding the elegant cigarette-lighter look-alike gun; and when he tested the trigger once, he half expected to see a little flame pop from the end.